EVERY SECOND
COUNTS

Visit us at www.boldstrokesbooks.com

By the Author

Bareback

Long Shot

Call Me Softly

Touch Me Gently

Every Second Counts

EVERY SECOND COUNTS

by

D. Jackson Leigh

2013

EVERY SECOND COUNTS

ISBN 10: 1-60282-785-0
ISBN 13: 978-1-60282-785-1

This Trade Paperback Original Is Published By
Bold Strokes Books, Inc.
P.O. Box 249
Valley Falls, NY 12185

First Edition: February 2013

CREDITS
Editor: Shelley Thrasher
Production Design: Susan Ramundo
Cover Design By Sheri (graphicartist2020@hotmail.com)

Acknowledgments

This book is special to me for many reasons, but mostly because it takes me back to several beginnings and the people who initially nudged me down this path to being a published author.

Marc Ryder, one of the main characters in this story, is a modern version of an old character very near and dear to my heart. The original cocky, risk-taking Rider—yes, spelled differently—was a character I developed when I began to tentatively test my fiction-writing skills in a role-playing Internet group. My first manuscript, *Bareback*, had been gathering dust for nearly five years when this group reignited my passion for writing. Two of my compatriots in the group were the very talented writers Cate Culpepper and Gill McKnight. With their prodding, I worked up the courage to submit *Bareback* to Bold Strokes Books, and the phone call I received three months later from BSB founder and CEO Len Barot was another beginning.

We talked about a lot of things during that phone call, but the most important was her question about my intentions. Bold Strokes was interested, she said, in signing and working with authors dedicated to constantly improving their skills. I vowed that I was, and she promised her team would help. Bold Strokes is more than living up to that commitment, and I like to think I am, too—that each book I write is better than the last.

That beginning led me to still another, my association with the very patient and insightful Shelley Thrasher. I trust her implicitly as my editor and count her and her wonderful partner, Connie, as good friends.

My final thanks goes to Angie, who was there at the beginning of it all, to the amazing supportive Bold Strokes family, and to my primo beta readers for *Every Second Counts*—Jenny Harmon, Carol Poynor, and Karen Belmar. Shelley said this is the cleanest manuscript I've ever given her. You rock.

Dedication

This book is dedicated to North Carolina National Guard Staff Sgt. Donna Johnson and her surviving spouse, Tracy Dice.

I will never forget meeting Tracy and the pride in her voice as she told me both she and her partner were members of the National Guard. She said she was buying my romance novels for Donna, who was currently deployed in Afghanistan. Two days later, Donna and two other Guardsmen were killed by a suicide bomber while on patrol.

This couple's sacrifice for their country, for all of us, is more than I can fathom and has touched me in a way I can't fully explain.

PROLOGUE

My name is Marc Ryder. I ride horses for money. I started out competing on the Grand Prix dressage circuit, but dressage felt too sedate, too controlled. So I jumped horses at Devon for two seasons, then wandered south and found brief respite from my restlessness on the polo fields of Wellington. The money was good and the competition fun, but I tired quickly of the Florida heat and decided to try steeplechase in Europe.

Steeplechase was exhilarating and reckless. But I was too tall and had to starve myself to be light enough to get the best rides at the top races. And, after a few years, the run-jump-run-jump grew repetitive, too.

Then, standing in Gatwick one day waiting for a flight to a race in Greece, I saw a real American cowboy. I took it as a sign because I am a professional rider. I sometimes ride airplanes to my next adventure.

So, I changed my ticket and managed to get a seat next to the guy. He was a rodeo rider, and we were headed to Texas.

I needed to put on thirty pounds of muscle to ride broncs and bulls, so I was relieved to be able to eat again. The novelty of a woman who could compete and win against the guys got me a lot of attention and several sponsors. I thought I'd finally found my calling until a particularly mean bull won me a long hospital stay and a leg full of metal pins.

That's how I ended up in the Dallas-Fort Worth airport, leaning on a cane and trying to decide whether I really wanted to board the plane to Cherokee Falls, Virginia. Home hadn't been on my itinerary for the past twelve years, but my former mentor, Skyler Reese, called to insist I return to the equestrian center to recuperate.

I had plenty of time, so I grabbed my duffel and settled on a bench to people-watch.

That's when I spotted her. Blond and blue-eyed, she wore the TSA uniform like it was tailored for her. Her shoulder-length hair and manicured nails kept her from being obvious, but something about the way she moved sent my gaydar pinging. I watched her direct the other security officers as they scanned the lines of people for possible terrorists and the carry-on bags for explosive devices.

She obviously was in charge. I like that in a woman.

Veteran flyer that I am, I know what triggers TSA suspicions. I purchased my ticket at the last minute. And, as I joined the impatient crowd filtering through the checkpoint, I pulled my ball cap low over my eyes and kept my sunglasses on. Also, I paused several times to let other people ahead of me. Even a rookie could tell I was maneuvering for the scanner operated by an employee spending more time talking than paying attention to his job. I could feel her watching.

I placed my duffel on the conveyer, threw my change and keys into a plastic tray, then limped forward. She was instantly at my side.

"Could you please remove your shoes and put them on the conveyor belt?"

I stared down at my Tony Lama boots as though baffled and then looked up at her. Her eyes were as blue as the Aegean Sea. I shrugged. "Can't."

"Everyone must remove their shoes to go through security."

"Can't you just X-ray them on my feet? I'll hop up on the belt and stick them under the scanner."

I was hoping for a smile, but her expression remained stoic. "No, I'm afraid we can't."

I tapped my cane against the brace wrapped around my left knee. "Pulling this boot off is a problem. I've got a bum knee. Can't bend it." It wasn't exactly true, but it sounded good enough.

"I'll get someone to assist you," she said.

Damn. I wanted *her* to assist me. Instead, she waved over a baby butch with a clip-on badge that identified her as a trainee. I hobbled to a nearby bench and the girl kneeled to carefully tug off my boot.

Blond and Beautiful held out her hand. "May I see your ID, please?"

I handed over my driver's license. She looked at it, then back at me. I thought I saw her eye twitch. She was having difficulty hiding her impatience.

"Would you please remove your glasses and cap, Mr. Ryder?"

I pulled off my cap and released my shoulder-length dark hair that had been tucked under it. Then I moved my sunglasses to a perch on top of my head and gave her a grin I knew would show off my dimples. Women love my dimples.

Her attitude changed from challenging to curious. "I apologize. Your license says Marc Ryder."

"My mother named me something awful, so I had it legally shortened to Marc when I turned eighteen. But everybody just calls me Ryder."

"Wow! You're Marc Ryder?" Baby Butch had returned from putting my boots on the conveyor. "Man, ESPN showed that bull stomping on you about a million times. When he tossed you up in the air…wow! Can I get your autograph? My friends are never going to believe I talked to you."

The kid obviously hadn't been trained yet in how to maintain that aloof TSA professional cool, so I held out my hand. "You have a pen?"

She patted her pockets but came up empty. Blond and Beautiful was using a nice black felt-tipped fine point to write my driver's-license number on her clipboard and Baby Butch stared hopefully at it.

"May I, Ms…?" I squinted at her badge. "Ms. Claire Simone?"

She reluctantly handed over the pen, and I scribbled my name across the bill of my cap that read EVERY SECOND COUNTS and handed it to Baby Butch. "Here ya go. I get these things free from one of my sponsors."

"Wow! Thanks."

Ms. Simone's eye definitely twitched that time. "If you would come this way, Ms. Ryder." She waved toward the metal detector. "Can you manage without the cane? It needs to go on the conveyor."

"I can manage if you help me a little." I was several inches taller, and she appeared startled when I happily flung my arm across her shoulders and leaned heavily on her. Truth was, I could walk very well without the cane, but she didn't know that. Christ, she smelled good. "What's that perfume you're wearing?"

"It's not a perfume. It's my moisturizer."

We paused to let a few other people rush through the detector first. I wasn't in a hurry to leave her company.

"Really? Where'd you get it? I need to buy a Christmas present for my sister." I, of course, didn't have a sister.

She hesitated. "Victoria's Secret."

I showed her my dimples again. "I love a woman who knows where to shop. What's the name of the lotion?"

She cleared her throat and mumbled, "Pure Seduction."

If I'd grinned any bigger, my face would've split. "It lives up to its name," I murmured in her ear before releasing her and hopping through the metal detector.

The alarms chirped in cadence with the happy pulsing of my clit and I obligingly assumed the stance, my arms held out to the side while the security officer moved his wand over my body. It beeped at the old steel plate in my forearm and the new metal pins in my leg.

Ms. Simone raised an elegant eyebrow. Damn, that was sexy. I shrugged and she handed over my cane when it emerged from the scanner. "I'm afraid I'll have to ask you to come with me for a full body scan."

Oh, yeah. I would've loved a full body scan by her, but I had even bigger plans. I followed her to the new scanner that had been causing such a stir in the media but stopped short of stepping behind the screen.

"I'm afraid I have to refuse."

"The machine is perfectly safe. You would receive more radiation from—"

"I'm sure I'm way over my limit for the year." I tapped my cane against my leg again for emphasis. "I've had more X-rays in the past two months than most people get their entire lifetime."

She seemed to consider my point. "Then you'll have to undergo a body search or we can't let you board the plane."

I looked over her shoulder. "A female officer will do it, right?"

"Yes, of course—" She whirled to gaze at the officers currently on duty. All men. She looked at Baby Butch, who flushed and licked her lips. Ms. Simone turned back to me. "I suppose I can do it, since I'm the only qualified female here."

I sighed dramatically. "Okay, but be gentle with me."

A sharp look from Ms. Simone cut Baby Butch's snicker short.

The three of us crowded into a small room and she shut the door. "Could you remove your sweatshirt, please?"

The thick hoodie draped low over my hips and was bulky enough to hide an Uzi. So, it was more than adequate for what I was concealing. When I peeled it off and dropped it to the floor, I was immensely pleased to detect a faint hitch in her breathing.

Her gaze traveled over my tight black racer-back tank, and my nipples came to attention, their salute more than obvious under the thin ribbed cotton. She glanced up and I gave her a sheepish smile and raised my arms for the anticipated grope. It didn't hurt that the position showed off the defined muscles in my arms and shoulders. I could tell she noticed.

She stepped back and looked into my eyes for a moment before dropping her gaze slowly down my lean torso. I cocked my hips slightly forward when she reached the bulge in my loose Wranglers. Her eyes jerked back up to my face and her expression shifted from amused to hungry. Oh, yeah. I'd read this one right.

She turned to pull two latex gloves from a box on the table. "Go to the supply room and get another box of gloves," she said to Baby Butch. "We're running low."

Baby Butch hesitated, glancing at the sign on the wall that read: TWO OFFICERS MUST BE PRESENT DURING BODY SEARCHES.

Taking advantage of Ms. Simone's apparent fascination with counting the remaining gloves, I jerked my chin in the direction of the door. Baby Butch took the hint and smirked. "Yes, ma'am. I'll go to the one on Concourse B. It was just restocked."

We were on Concourse C and I gave her a wink of approval as she made her exit.

"May I call you Claire? I like to be on a first-name basis with the women who feel me up."

She didn't answer, but I could see a hint of a smile.

She started with my hair, gently running her fingers over my scalp, then across my shoulders and down my arms. I guess I could've been hiding a knife or something explosive under my bare skin. I watched her face and wished she wasn't wearing gloves. I imagined her hands soft and warm on me.

She stepped closer to search down my back. When she moved to my front, I didn't even try to suppress the groan as she ran her hands several times up and down, pressing firmly over my hard nipples as required. She blushed an attractive pink.

I felt an answering flush rise up my neck, too, when she knelt and palmed my butt cheeks. I'm sure that little squeeze isn't standard protocol. Her hands moved quickly down the back and outside of my legs, then slowly up the inside of my thighs. I widened my stance and wondered if she could smell how wet I was.

I looked down to hold her gaze as her knuckles brushed my crotch and bumped against the contraband concealed there.

"Do you have something in your pocket, Ms. Ryder?"

"It's not in my pocket." I couldn't help that my voice had dropped to a low purr. She had that effect on me.

She stood and my clit jumped again as her fingers gripped my waistband and gently tugged upward as though measuring the weight of it.

"It's a…prosthesis," I explained. "There's no metal in it, so the easiest way to get it through security is to wear it. It's something I enjoy when I find the right person to share it with."

Her eyes darkened and she palmed the hard ridge, pushing it against my pulsing sex. "I'm afraid I'll have to confirm what it is, of course."

I couldn't stop the spasm that ran through my gut and thrust my pelvis into her hands. "I understand," I whispered hoarsely.

She slowly lowered my zipper and wrapped her fingers around the dildo's girth, pumping gently. I closed my eyes and whimpered, thoroughly blowing my smooth act. I'm not sure how she'd turned the tables so easily, but I prayed I wouldn't embarrass myself by popping off right there. I was so close. I blew out a breath as she withdrew and raised my zipper.

"Seems harmless," she said, fastening the button on my jeans but keeping her fingers tucked into my waistband.

I struggled against a sudden desire to kiss her, to plunge my tongue past her perfect lips. Instead, I confessed.

"I can guarantee it's not harmless," I said. "In fact, it has been known to cause…explosions."

The back of her hand subtly rubbed against my hard belly.

"Then this…prosthesis…may be something the TSA would like to research more. Do you live in the area, Ms. Ryder?"

"Just leaving. Going to Virginia for the short term. It doesn't mean I won't be coming back. Do you live here, Claire?"

She shook her head ruefully. "No. I live in DC. I'm in town for another week to train staff on how to use the new body scanners." She stepped back, releasing me. "Enjoy your flight."

I shrugged. "I'm afraid I've missed my plane. It could be several days before I can catch another."

She looked at me, her blue eyes hooded. "I can recommend the hotel just down the road. That's where I'm staying."

I leaned so close our lips were almost touching. I could feel her breath on my face. "It sounds perfect, if you'll have dinner with me after you get off work."

"I suppose I could. There is that research—"

"And I'll be happy to assist you."

Did I mention I'm a professional rider? Sometimes I ride simply for pleasure.

CHAPTER ONE

"Next up, Marc Ryder, currently in second place. She'll be throwing a leg over number five-seven-five, Funeral Wagon, for her third and final ride of the day."

The announcer's voice rose over the excited yells of the audience and echoed through the sound system of the indoor coliseum.

Sweat trickled down Ryder's jaw and into her collar. She climbed down the steel bars of the chute and gently brushed her boot against the spine of the two-thousand-pound, solid black bull to let him know she was there. The bull bellowed and threw his body against the sides of the narrow stall, angrily clanging his horns along the metal.

The animal was already lathered with sweat, and its pungent odor combined with the dust of the arena to coat her sinuses and throat. She coughed and spit into the dirt, then breathed it all in again. God, she loved the rodeo—every primal smell, every adrenaline-pumping ride, and every beautiful groupie in tight Wranglers and fancy boots.

"Take your time," the stock steward said, interrupting her thoughts.

She pulled her Stetson down tight and cocked her head to wink at him. "Piece of cake, Randy."

He shook his head. "I think this one got up on the wrong side of the barn today, Ryder. We couldn't even get him in the chute earlier."

She already knew that. She could be riding Bushwhacker. She had the option to request that this bull be sent back to the barn and the entire lineup shifted forward. But being the only woman in the competition meant that even after four years and earning a top-ten ranking, she still had to prove herself.

"This big guy's going to put me in the money," she said.

She was confident this angry black bull with his four-foot span of horns and ominous name could give her the ride she needed to cinch second place, a personal best, and her ticket to the National Rodeo Finals.

"He's gonna break your neck. Women are supposed to ride horses, not bulls," Randy muttered.

She wasn't offended. Randy was one of the few men who gave her the respect she was due on the circuit. His remark was just his awkward way of expressing his frustration at her nonchalance.

He locked eyes with her. "I'm just saying, when you get off this one, you better hightail it outta there 'cause he's gonna be looking for trouble."

"That's the plan."

She took a deep breath and slid smoothly onto the broad back. This time, the bull went still, tensing like a coiled spring. Her seat was the only part of her jeans not protected by her leather chaps, and the wet heat of the beast's body soaked through to her skin. She fought the instinct to tighten her legs while she went through her ritual of pulling the bull rope taut, situating her right hand into its handle, and tightly wrapping its braided leather tail around her palm. She used her left hand to pound her gloved fingers into the rosin-coated braid for a firmer grip.

The bull snorted but remained steady as she inched forward until her crotch touched the back of her hand and her legs were securely in front of the bull rope. She took a rubber mouth guard from her pocket and popped it between her teeth.

She stared at the back of the bull's massive head for a long moment as the noise from the crowd, anticipating the signal for release, reached a deafening crescendo.

A deep breath and she gave a quick nod.

Funeral Wagon leapt out of the gate, twisting and kicking his hind legs high and to the right in a high-scoring sunfish move.

One second.

He crow-hopped hard on his front legs in a jarring effort to throw her forward, then sunfished again in the other direction. It was a trick that could unseat a broad-shouldered man, but, as a woman, her center of gravity was lower and she moved easily with the animal.

Three seconds.

She raked her dulled spurs along the bull's tough hide for extra points as he bucked through several high kicks.

Four seconds.

He launched into a prolonged bucking spin, but she carefully avoided the temptation to lean too far inside and get "sucked into the well."

Six seconds.

An abrupt change of direction, then a third sunfish nearly unseated her. Christ, it felt like her shoulder was separating, and the muscles in her forearm were stretched tight enough to snap. Still, she gritted her teeth and tightened her grip.

Seven seconds.

The next few bucks were straight up and down, so she laid back and again worked her spurs.

Eight seconds!

The buzzer sounded loud across the arena as the bull gathered his feet under him for one last mighty heave. She loosened her grip and waited for the right second to jump free. Rather than shifting back when he kicked his heels high into the air, she hunched forward to push off the massive shoulders.

She glanced down to confirm that her hand had slipped free of the bull rope, and when she looked up again, the massive horn-crowned head of Funeral Wagon filled her vision.

She realized her mistake a split second too late.

Ryder jerked awake, her heart pounding. She sat up and blinked at her surroundings, then rubbed her clammy, shaking hands along her denim-covered thighs.

She wasn't in the arena. She wasn't waking up in a hospital. She was in an airplane. That wasn't a heart monitor beeping. It was Claire tapping her nails on the armrest as she read her magazine.

She swallowed the nauseating fear that threatened to empty the contents of her stomach and concentrated on taking slow, deep breaths.

Claire glanced up from her magazine. "Good dream, huh? Last time I heard you breathing that hard was, oh, about five hours ago… in the shower, before we had to leave for the airport."

Ryder licked her dry lips. "Yeah. I was, uh, reliving the shower scene."

The seatbelt sign flashed on and the stewardess announced their imminent arrival in Richmond, Virginia, so they buckled up and readied to land. Claire turned, her mouth close to Ryder's ear.

"You certainly turned a boring assignment in Dallas into a week I won't soon forget." She nipped Ryder's earlobe. "Since we're arriving early, I've got about forty-five minutes before I have to board my next flight. I happen to know a nice, secluded spot in this airport for one more good-bye."

Perfect. She needed to get her head out of that arena and back where it should be—between a sexy pair of legs.

Chapter Two

W here the hell is she?" Skyler Reese, director of the Cherokee Falls Young Equestrian Program, propped against the wall and eyed the luggage moving along the conveyor, while veterinarian Tory Greyson scanned the thinning crowd in the baggage claim area of the Richmond International Airport.

"I don't know. But if she's a no-show this time, she can rent a damn car to get back to Cherokee Falls," Tory said. "I'm not rearranging my schedule a third time for her sorry ass."

"You had to pick up that semen shipment anyway."

Tory glanced down at the cooler protectively tucked between her feet. "I could have sent my intern to pick this up. Hell, it's for breeding mares at your barn. I should've just let you pick it up."

Skyler elbowed her. "Admit it. You can't wait to see her either."

They had been a gang of three as teens, the most promising riders at the Cherokee Falls Equestrian Center and the most likely to find trouble.

Often mistaken for sisters, Skyler and Tory were both tall and blond, with similar short, layered haircuts. Their eyes told their difference. Skyler's were sepia-toned and brooding, Tory's pine-forest-green and welcoming.

Their pasts were just as opposite.

Skyler came from an abusive home and rose to fame as a gold-medalist equestrian, only to be blacklisted from the eventing circuit for sleeping with the wrong woman. She re-established her career as a trainer and found her salvation in her partner, Jessica Parker-Reese, heiress to the equestrian center and Parker fortune that funded the program Skyler ran for troubled kids.

Tory grew up in a loving Catholic family and followed a traditional life path of attending college and veterinary school, and then establishing her own business. She had been the voice of reason in Skyler's and Ryder's schemes, the one who stepped aside when Jessica explained she could only be a friend because—like many of Tory's past girlfriends—she'd fallen for Skyler. She had been the one to always forgive and forget. That was, until she met Leah Montgomery and found the voice to fight for what she wanted, who she needed.

Ryder was the latecomer to the group. Several years younger, she was dark-haired and more physically compact, gregarious, volatile and adventure-seeking. She was the one who'd wandered away from Cherokee Falls to find her fortune.

Yet, with all their differences, spending their formative years together had forged an unbreakable bond.

Tory scowled, then smiled and shook her head. "You're right. It's past time for the third Musketeer to come home."

"Damn right. That's exactly what I said when I called her and told her to get her ass back here."

Tory was quiet for a minute. "I saw the YouTube clip of that bull goring and stomping her. Scared the hell out of me."

"Yeah, me too, Tor." Skyler narrowed her eyes. She strode quickly to the conveyor and snatched up a large black duffel embroidered with rodeo patches and red italic stitching that proclaimed, EVERY SECOND COUNTS.

"That's her sponsor's logo. It's got to be her bag," Tory said.

Skyler checked the identification tag attached to the handle by a length of braided rawhide. "Yep. It's hers." They resettled against the wall. "Doesn't mean she got on the plane."

They waited a few more minutes.

"Let's go upstairs and see if they can confirm she was on board," Tory said. "If she is here, she won't be going anywhere without this."

Skyler was about to agree when several loud thumps sounded. They turned to stare at the wall behind them. Silence. Skyler dismissed the noise with a shrug.

"We should try the VIP lounge. As much traveling as she does, she's gotta be a member," Tory said.

"Good idea. She's probably up there, putting the moves on some woman while we wait down here. I'm gonna kill her." Skyler bent to pick up the duffel and another noise filtered through the wall. This time it was a low moan, followed by "Yeah, babe." A higher-pitched whimper answered. "Inside, I want you inside." A pause, then a solid thump.

Damn, that wall was thin.

"I love how wet you get for me. Slides right in."

Skyler blinked. That voice sounded strangely familiar.

"Wrap your legs around my hips. I can hold you up."

"But your knee—"

"It's fine. Just relax, babe, and enjoy the ride."

"Oh, God. Oh, yeah. That's right. Give me a fuck I won't forget."

Scuffling noises changed to the softer sound of something bumping gently against the wall in a steady cadence. Another whimper.

Skyler shook her head and motioned for Tory to follow. A sign forbade all except authorized personnel, but the door wasn't locked. They slipped inside, closing it quietly behind them.

The long, wide hallway was empty and a door to their immediate left was marked STORAGE. Skyler took up sentry on one side of it and indicated for Tory to do the same on the other.

Wait, Skyler mouthed silently.

Ryder dropped to one knee and impatiently ran her hands up Claire's smooth thighs. She pushed the tight skirt up to Claire's waist and growled. "I love a woman who doesn't wear panty hose...or anything else underneath."

Her mouth watered at the heady scent of Claire's arousal, and she plunged her tongue into the neatly trimmed curls without ceremony. After all, they'd spent nearly the entire past week getting intimately acquainted with every part of each other's body.

She had hoped for a restful, solitary plane ride from Dallas but didn't protest when Claire announced that she'd managed to route her return trip to DC through Richmond so they could have a bit more time together. After a week of nonstop hot monkey sex, Ryder owed her that. Right?

The minute they lifted off that Dallas runway, Claire's hand had found Ryder's thigh, her long red nails scraping the inside seam of Ryder's loose jeans and creeping under the hem of her baggy hoodie to grasp and stroke the dildo strapped to her hips. By the time they'd landed, Ryder was slick and hard and pulsing.

So she'd eagerly followed when Claire led her through the maze of interior corridors to this storage room and whispered, "One last ride, stud."

Claire's scent filling her nose and her juices coating her tongue, she stood and Claire dropped to *her* knees, fumbling to open Ryder's jeans and slide them down her hips. Ryder was commando, too, except for the harness and dildo, and her thighs were dripping with her own arousal. Claire looked up and tongued the dildo. Ryder groaned. Claire slid her hand between Ryder's rock-hard thighs and plunged her fingers into her, deep and hard.

"Yeah, babe."

Claire tongued the dildo again but withdrew and stood. "Inside. I want you inside."

Ryder pinned Claire against the wall and nudged her legs apart. She refused to acknowledge the pain that shot through her left leg as she bent her knees and pushed the full length of her cock in.

"I love how wet you get for me." She lifted Claire's thighs. "Wrap your legs around me. I can hold you up."

"But your knee—"

"It's fine. Just relax, babe, and enjoy the ride."

"Oh, God. Oh, yeah. That's right. Give me a fuck I won't forget."

She drew back and drove forward to set up a steady rhythm she knew would bring them both to a quick climax. Claire had a plane to catch and she had friends to meet. Ryder rolled her hips with each upward thrust to grind against Claire's sex and rub the dildo's base along her own hard clit. Claire's arms tightened around her neck and her heels dug into Ryder's butt as if she couldn't get her deep enough, hard enough inside.

"That's right, babe. Ride me good."

"Oh, oh. I'm gonna come."

Ryder groaned when Claire snaked one hand under the hoodie and found her breast. The hard, twisting pinch sent a jolt of electricity to her crotch. She gritted her teeth and fought to hold back her orgasm.

Claire's whimpers turned into a keening whine and she arched against the wall. She shuddered through her climax, but before the tremors stopped, Ryder pulled out and spun her around.

"God, you've got a great ass." She bit down on one smooth cheek, her teeth eliciting a surprised squeak. Then she pressed her chest against Claire's back to bend her over and took Claire's hands to place them against the wall. "Brace yourself, babe, this ride's not over."

She grabbed Claire's hips and again plunged inside. This position was a lot easier on her injured leg and she drove her cock relentlessly, savoring the slap of her flesh against Claire's ass.

"Oh, God." Claire spread her legs wider and arched up to meet Ryder's pumping hips. "Oh, God."

Injured or not, Ryder's legs were like steel bands and, as her orgasm gathered, her thrusts lifted Claire onto her toes with each stroke. She felt for Claire's breast and squeezed the nipple hard. She couldn't hold off this time, so she slid her fingers over Claire's clit, stretched tight by the cock boring into her, and stroked it firmly. Claire clamped a hand over her own mouth and screamed her climax into it.

Ryder groaned and bucked through her orgasm. "Fuck, yeah. Oh, yeah."

They panted for a long minute, Claire still bent over and Ryder pressed against her back. When their breathing slowed, Ryder pulled her cock free and Claire moaned with the movement.

Ryder glanced around at the surrounding shelves. Nothing but jugs of industrial cleaner. She pulled off her hoodie and tank top underneath, offering the soft undershirt to Claire to dry off a bit. But Claire shook her head and daintily pulled a mini-pack of wipes from her purse to clean up before straightening her skirt. Ryder shrugged and wiped the undershirt between her own legs and along the dildo before tugging her jeans up and slipping back into her hoodie. She rolled the sticky tank up and stuffed it into the hoodie's pouch.

Claire glanced at her watch. "Damn, I've got to hurry or I'm going to miss my flight."

"Yeah, and my friends are probably looking—" Ryder opened the door and bumped into a tall roadblock. "Oh, well, guess they found me." She grinned up at Skyler. "Hey, guys. Hope I didn't keep you waiting long."

Claire glanced at the two women, then turned to Ryder. "I should be embarrassed, but I don't have time." She pulled her down for a long, tongue-filled kiss. "Thanks for an unforgettable week, stud. You've got my numbers if you're ever in DC." One last peck on the lips and she was sprinting down the corridor as fast as her three-inch heels would carry her.

Ryder grinned at Skyler and Tory, and shrugged. "That was Claire. She's an FAA official."

Tory tossed the black duffel into Ryder's arms and arched an eyebrow.

"Would you believe we met when she strip-searched me in Dallas?" Ryder glanced down the hallway where Claire had disappeared. "She was, uh, the unexpected delay in my flight plans."

"I'd believe just about anything where you're concerned," Skyler said, grabbing the shoulder of Ryder's hoodie and dragging her toward the exit.

Tory's nostrils flared and she wrinkled her nose. "Christ, you smell like a brothel. You're not getting in my truck until we stop by a restroom and you stuff that thing you're packing into your bag and wash up."

Ryder laughed. "Still campaigning for the nunnery, huh, Tory?"

Damn, it was good to see them again. They fell back into their familiar roles as if they'd never been apart—Skyler the alpha, Ryder the restless, and Tory the pure-hearted, who was the glue that held the three of them together. "It's okay. You two are getting up in age. I don't mind handling the hot ones for ya."

Skyler hooted and grabbed Ryder in a good-natured headlock. "I see that bull's horn didn't puncture your ego, half-pint."

"Stop it, you Neanderthal." Ryder extricated herself from Skyler's grip. "I can't believe you're still calling me that. You guys are only a few inches taller than me."

Skyler cocked her head at Tory. "What do you think? Should we let her test her skills on your Tennessee firecracker?"

Tory grinned at the mention of her feisty partner. "Now, that's just mean. The kid's already injured, Skyler. Leah would cut her to shreds."

Ryder strutted between them. "Bring her on. No woman alive can resist the old Ryder charm."

Skyler shoved her toward the restroom entrance. "You keep thinking that, half-pint. Tory and I will be around to pick you up when you find your ass in the dirt with seven seconds to go before the buzzer."

CHAPTER THREE

A determined songster in a nearby tree and the scrape of Bridgette LeRoy's charcoal pencil across her sketchpad were the only sounds as she worked to capture the antics of Sure Thing, a midnight-black Chincoteague pony, cavorting with a larger yearling in the pasture below her. The slightly overcast morning provided perfect lighting as she sat on the trunk of her car and observed the two colts in their mock battle over a herd of imaginary mares.

The larger colt clumsily half reared and pushed forward to knock Sure off-balance with his heavier weight. But the Chincoteague was fast and agile. He leapt to the side and reared high to plant his front hooves against his friend's shoulder.

Bridgette drew quickly, ignoring detail to outline a panel of poses. She congratulated herself. She couldn't wait to show Leah. This was good.

Her life was good. She'd been skeptical when her cousin, Cheryl, called her about a teaching position open at Earnhardt College. She had always been a world traveler, a vagabond artist, but had reached a point in her life where she needed something constant, something solid. So she applied for the job and discovered that she loved teaching budding artists.

When Bridgette moved to Cherokee Falls, Tory became her first friend, a friend with intimate benefits. The nature of their relationship changed, however, when Leah captured Tory's heart. Although the sex between Tory and her had been hot and wonderful, Bridgette was fine giving that up for a more traditional friendship because she couldn't offer her heart as Leah did.

Despite her past with Tory, she and Leah became friends, too. They also were business partners in a very successful series of children's books with Sure as the subject. Leah, the writer, usually came up with the ideas and the words, but Bridgette was delighted to be able to supply the subject of their next story. She could easily develop the figures on her paper into a lesson on bullying.

The colts' joust lasted a few more minutes before it became a game of tag and they disappeared over a hill at a full gallop. With the yearlings gone, Bridgette began to fill in detail while her memory was still fresh. She was thoroughly absorbed when a piercing whistle jerked her attention from her work.

The thirty acres behind East Barn were divided into three pastures, each extending outward from the building to allow easy access to different groups of horses. In the narrow pasture that ran up to the back of the barn, a figure stood inside the fence.

Bridgette stared. Dark hair just touching the shoulders implied that the person was female, but the muscular shoulders encased in a form-fitting black T-shirt seemed to belong to a lean teen-aged boy.

The boy raised his hand to his mouth and released another sharp whistle.

A white Arabian appeared at the top of the rise and stopped. The horse stared down at the source of the summons and then lifted its nose to test the morning air.

"Walker!"

The horse twitched his ears forward and then charged down the hill at a full gallop, his tail a flag held high in the wind.

Bridgette flipped to a clean page and began to draw, glancing up between strokes of her pencil to capture the scene as it unfolded.

The stallion was a testament to his Arabian ancestry, the oldest and purest blood stock in the world and the tap root of so many other equine breeds. Strong withers led to an elegant neck, and his broad forehead tapered down to a delicate muzzle with large nostrils. His sleek body shimmered as the clouds broke and the sun touched his snowy coat.

Then, as suddenly as he began his charge, the stallion halted several feet from the boy, scenting and blowing to confirm the identity of the interloper. He cautiously sniffed the offered hand. His ears worked back and forth, and then he rumbled a low greeting and stepped forward to gently bump his head against the boy's chest.

The breeze carried low, indistinguishable words. The boy stroked and then wrapped his arms around the stallion's arched neck. After a moment, the boy stepped back and wiped his hands over his cheeks. Grabbing a handful of mane, he leapt onto the stallion's back.

The horse wheeled and ran so fast, Bridgette half expected him to unfurl wings and take off into the sky. But he stayed aground, his rider hunched low against his neck, urging him faster until they were suddenly gone.

It was so magical, Bridgette marveled at how easy it would be to believe that they, indeed, had disappeared into a cloud rather than over the pasture's ridge.

"That must be Skyler's and Tory's friend."

Absorbed in her drawing, Bridgette jumped at the voice but smiled when she turned to its source.

"Sorry, I thought you heard me drive up." Jessica propped her hip against the warm metal of the car. She gestured toward one of the golf-cart-sized utility vehicles they used to travel among the five barns at the nationally ranked training facilities of the Cherokee Falls Equestrian Center. She and Skyler were partners in life and in business. Jessica managed the training center, and Skyler devoted her time to their program for troubled kids.

"I was too absorbed in what I was drawing." Bridgette rested her sketchpad in her lap. "What did you say?"

"I was wondering if that was the friend Skyler and Tory went to pick up in Richmond. Did you talk to her?" Jessica's pale-blue eyes scanned the ridge for the rider.

"That was a woman on the stallion?" *Hmmm.* "I don't think she saw me. You haven't met her?"

"No. I was taking a nap when they got back from the airport. I guess Sky didn't want to wake me." Jessica sighed and absently rubbed her belly, eight-months swollen with the daughter she and Skyler anxiously awaited. "This little one takes all my energy."

Although Bridgette had never contemplated pregnancy herself, Jessica truly glowed with it. "I'm surprised Skyler went all the way to Richmond. Leah said she hardly lets you out of her sight these days."

Jessica laughed. "She really wanted to go, so I promised I would rest while they were gone, and Leah swore she would be only a phone call away."

"So you haven't met their friend before?" The boyish physique intrigued Bridgette.

"No. Sky said the three of them were running buddies when they were kids, but she hasn't been back to Cherokee Falls for more than ten years."

"That horse seemed to know her."

"That's her stallion that's been boarding here the whole time. Sky said she raised him from a baby, but I'm surprised he remembered her since she's been out of town so long."

Bridgette shaded her eyes and looked out across the pasture. "What brings her back here now? The horse?"

"An injury. She's a professional rider." Jessica looked down at the knee Bridgette knew held the titanium joint that had ended her riding career. "I know what that's like. I don't think she has any family or a partner, so I told Sky to call her up and insist she come here to rehab."

Bridgette frowned. She hadn't noticed an injury when the woman swung up on the horse and rode off at a gallop.

"Anyway, Sky left a note saying they'd be at Creek Barn breeding some mares, and I was headed over there when I saw you. Leah's coming over later and we're grilling steaks to welcome our guest. Can you join us?"

Bridgette closed her sketchpad. "I'd love to, but I've got a faculty meeting in an hour and a class to teach tonight."

"Too bad." Jessica wiggled her eyebrows. "I understand she's something of a charmer."

The woman had been too far away for Bridgette to see her face clearly, but she did find athletic women particularly attractive. "How long will she be here?"

"I haven't talked to her yet, but I'm sure it'll be at least a couple of months."

Bridgette tossed her pad and chalks into the car. "Sorry I can't stay, but I need to get going or I'll be late to the meeting."

Jessica stepped back from the car. "Come find me next time you're out here and I'll introduce you. You two might hit it off."

She chuckled. Matchmaking was a burden all single lesbians had to endure. "Maybe I'll do that. Say hey to everybody for me."

❖

Except for the reason behind it, Bridgette would have been grateful for the somber mood of the faculty meeting because it matched her own frame of mind. She'd been uncharacteristically unsettled lately. Perhaps the underlying uncertainty that had infused the college campus in recent months had caused it. Rumors of deep cuts in the college's art department had been circulating and were the anticipated subject of this emergency gathering.

William Blanchard, the department chairman, worked his way through his colleagues and stood at the end of the long conference table. "Please, everybody find a seat. I won't take too much time."

"I hope we're going to talk about how sweltering the studios were this summer," the woman next to Bridgette said. "I know we're having a budget crisis, but my students couldn't work with sweat dripping onto their sketches, and they won't be able to do anything this winter if their hands are numb from cold."

William ignored her and cleared his throat. "I just came from a meeting with the chancellor and the news isn't good."

He waited while murmurs rippled through the group.

"Enrollment is down over the past two years because student financial aid is declining at the federal and state levels. General fund-raising is off at least twenty percent, and several of our endowment's more aggressive investments tanked with the market."

"I knew hiring that young idiot of a chancellor would be the end of us."

Bridgette wasn't sure who spoke, but they all were thinking that.

William held up his hand. "Chancellor Waite did gamble a bit, but we're in no worse shape than most other private institutions. We're all suffering."

"Just give us the bottom line, William. How big's the cut?" asked Wesley Grant, a tenured professor whose job was secure unless the entire college closed. Bridgette was an artist-in-residence, a program that, while valued, would be on the chopping block long before a tenured position. She wasn't sure she wanted to hear what was coming.

"Next year, the college will fund the positions of only tenured faculty and one administrator." He had to raise his voice over the angry din. "And the rest of the art-department budget will be cut twenty percent."

"We can't operate like that."

"That's insane."

"We'll lose more students."

The protests quieted when Jonathan Frank stood. A widely respected senior member of the faculty, the tall, white-haired sculptor had a quiet but commanding presence.

"The art department is the foundation of this institution. Earnhardt College may be small, but it was built on our reputation. And this department has enjoyed international recognition because of our diverse faculty." He paused to scan the faces of his fellow faculty. "We said nothing when this new chancellor reallocated our art resources to other departments because he wanted to 'broaden our appeal.' We gave up a third of our studio space to new science labs. We broadened our class offerings to accommodate non-art majors." He fastened a scathing glare on poor William. "Enough. This is not acceptable."

Everyone looked at William expectantly.

"I'm sorry, Jon. What you say is very true, but my hands are tied. The board of trustees supports Chancellor Waite. Drastic times mean drastic measures."

Bridgette frowned. Although her art sales and investments provided most of her income, she loved teaching. She could find a teaching position at another institution, but she had made friends and found a home here in Cherokee Falls. She looked around the table. "Surely we can do something."

William stood to take the floor again and Jonathan sank back into his seat. "Yes, we can raise our own endowment, independent of the college. We will fund our own teaching positions and pay our own staff."

Someone grumbled. "Easier said than done."

"Dr. Blanchard is right," Bridgette said. "This department has produced some very notable artists, whom some of you sitting around this table have mentored." She pushed her chair back and stood. "Surely they wouldn't let their alma mater suffer these dire cuts without offering to help."

Her colleagues' faces showed a mix of emotions.

"Are you suggesting that we beg from our former students?"

"I signed up to teach art, not whore for Earnhardt College."

"Asking for money is so belittling."

Bridgette held up her hand for silence. "We don't have to solicit money. We can ask for art donations, hold an auction, and pledge the proceeds to the new endowment. It won't be enough, of course, but it's a start."

"That's an excellent idea, Ms. LeRoy." William slapped his hands together. "I'm appointing you chairwoman. Jonathan, Amelia, and Justin, you also are on the committee to get this off the ground. Now, you'll have to excuse me. I have a meeting in a few minutes with an art patron. Instead of asking for money, maybe I'll ask for something from his collection for this auction."

Bridgette pushed her way through the other faculty members— milling about and complaining about the meeting's abrupt end—and hurried to catch up with William.

"Dr. Blanchard, wait. Surely you'd want to appoint someone more senior in the department. I've only been here a little over two years. I don't want to cause any hard feelings."

She followed him into the elevator and the doors slid shut as he pressed the button for the first floor.

"In case you didn't catch on, most members of the senior faculty consider fund-raising an odious task. They'll be happy to let you do the work." He sighed. "I'm more worried that Jonathan and Justin will give you precious little help beyond contacting the few former students they've mentored. Hopefully, Amelia will assist you with the details. Women are so much better than men at planning events."

Bridgette resisted rolling her eyes. It irritated her that men liked to claim masculine shortcomings as an excuse for laziness.

The elevator doors opened and they stepped into the long lobby where an impressive gallery of artwork was on display. William stopped and gazed around him, as if taking one last look.

"I've spent the past fifteen years, as have many department chairmen before me, collecting the artwork displayed in this building. I consider it my life's greatest accomplishment."

He rubbed at his temple. For the first time, Bridgette realized the weight of the burden this man carried for all of them.

"I'd lobby to sell every damned precious piece of it if that would save this school." His voice wavered and he paused to clear his throat. "But, technically, it belongs to the college, not the art school. It's part of our institutional assets that secure the college's bond rating."

He turned to Bridgette, his gaze determined. "You have good ideas, current contacts in New York, and, despite your short time here, the respect of your fellow artists. I'm counting on you to help us, Ms. LeRoy."

Bridgette stared at his back as he walked away. He hesitated at the open door and turned to her. "Perhaps you'd like to start by painting or sculpting something for the auction. Prime the pump, so to speak." He didn't wait for her answer.

She plopped down on a nearby bench and rested her head in her hands. Other than the children's books she'd been illustrating, she hadn't produced a single marketable piece in the past two years. Saving the art school might be easier than curing her recent dry spell.

CHAPTER FOUR

Y ou might want to lighten up on the beer until you eat something."

The late-afternoon sun that had been warming her almost blinded Ryder when she opened her eyes, and she squinted to focus on Tory standing over her.

"I'm okay. Just tired. Long day."

"Leg okay? I see you've put the brace back on."

"Yeah. I probably shouldn't have taken it off for that little ride on Wind Walker, but I had a pain pill a little while ago. It's kicking in now."

"Like I said, you may want to slow down on the beer until we eat. Steaks are done. We're just waiting for Leah to get here with the potato salad."

Ryder sat up straighter in the chaise lounge. "If I pass out, just throw a blanket over me. This chair is pretty comfortable."

Tory dropped into the chair next to her. "I've got no problem doing that, but Jess would make me or Skyler carry your sorry butt all the way upstairs."

"Yes, I would," Jessica said from where she had been resting on the chaise next to Ryder's.

The back door slammed and Skyler joined them, holding out a denim overshirt to Jessica.

"Sun's going down. I didn't want you to get chilled," she said.

Jessica smiled up at her. "Thanks, sweetie, but between the hot flashes and this furnace that's taken up residence in my belly, I don't need it right now." She sat up and scooted forward in the chair. "I do need a human pillow since you're finished grilling the steaks."

Skyler dropped the shirt into an empty chair and slid her long body into the requested spot. Ryder watched them as Jessica leaned back against Skyler with a contented sigh, and Skyler wrapped her arms around her very pregnant partner to caress her oversized abdomen.

"Is she kicking much today?"

Jessica snorted. "Like a soccer player. One more month."

"I love you," Skyler murmured, kissing Jessica's cheek. "I love you for doing this for us."

"Even when I'm fat and cranky?"

"You're not fat. You're pregnant, and it's a very sexy look for you."

Jessica laughed. "You keep saying that, but I'll be glad to get back to my former self once this little girl decides to make her debut." She pulled Skyler's hand up to kiss the palm. "Did you remember to put the clothes where I can reach them?"

"Yes. And I folded them for you."

"You didn't have to do that, honey. I could have folded them. I just can't bend down to get them out of the dryer any more. But thank you."

Ryder frowned. This wasn't the Skyler Reese that used to be her running buddy. That Skyler had made bets with her on who could bed the most women at a three-day horse show. She was the only woman Ryder knew who had more notches in her bedpost than she did. This was some stranger who hosted cookouts and, God almighty, folded clothes.

Maybe it was a mistake to come back to Cherokee Falls to recuperate. Her friends' priorities had obviously changed, and she was feeling very out of place.

But when Skyler had called and invited her, it seemed like a much better option than sitting around her Dallas condo staring at the walls for three months while she completed her physical therapy. Right now, she wasn't so sure what would be worse, staring at condo walls or seeing her lioness mentor behave like a house cat.

A white BMW pulled up, and a petite brunette got out and leaned over the convertible's back door to lift a large bowl from the backseat. What a great ass. The woman turned toward them. A beauty, too.

"Potato salad's here." Tory stood.

"More like dessert." Ryder stood, too. This was what she needed—some familiar fun. "Who's that?"

"That's Leah, my—"

"Jess and Leah have been friends since they were kids." Skyler cut Tory off with a subtle shake of her head. "She's the Texas firecracker we mentioned at the airport. Remember? That's when you said there wasn't a woman alive who could resist your charm."

"Skyler." Jessica's voice held a stern warning. "You shouldn't—"

Ryder laughed and put her hand out. "It's okay. I've got this."

Tory started to protest, too, then shrugged and settled back into her chair. "Do your best, tiger."

Since the pain pill was making her a little fuzzy, she gave herself a few seconds to steady and then started toward the car.

Jessica called after her. "Cane."

"Shit." Ryder caught the offensive prop when Tory tossed it to her and hobbled along as nonchalantly as possible with a brace on her leg.

"They told me someone else would be joining us, but they didn't warn me how beautiful she would be," Ryder said as she approached. "I'm Marc Ryder, but everybody calls me Ryder."

"Well, aren't you sweet? I'm Leah Montgomery." Leah balanced the heavy bowl on the top of the door and extended her hand.

Ryder soaked her in. Hot as a Texas blacktop with an accent as thick and smooth as Southern Comfort. She'd hit the jackpot. She brought Leah's hand to her lips and smiled at her. "Can I help you with that?"

"That's very gallant, but I'll carry the potato salad since you only have one available hand. It's kind of heavy. You can get the baby gift from the backseat."

Ryder easily scooped the bowl up with her free hand. "It's not a problem."

"I guess it's not for a big, tough rodeo rider." Leah ran her hand along Ryder's arm and squeezed the hard bicep. Her gaze was predatory. Ryder liked that.

"You know about that, huh?"

"I lived in Dallas for a while before I moved to Virginia. Besides, it's hard to live around here and not know about the woman from Cherokee Falls who's the only female to ever successfully ride bulls."

It was difficult to strut in a brace, but Ryder did her best as they returned to the group. She set the bowl on the patio table and waited while Leah laid the baby gift next to it. Then she offered her arm and grinned when Leah slipped her hand around her bicep again.

"My goodness, you must work out a lot." Leah purred like a cat.

Ryder led her over to where the rest of the group was waiting and indicated the chaise where she'd been lounging. "Why don't you sit here and I'll take the end, so we can get to know each other."

"Oh, I would, darlin', if I didn't already have a reserved seat." She gave Ryder's bicep another squeeze. "You're so cute, going all Romeo on me." She turned to Tory. "Isn't she, baby?" She dropped into Tory's lap. "But you, stud, are the one I've been missing all day. You left our bed before dawn this morning." She cupped Tory's face in her hands and gave her a long, deep kiss.

Ryder dropped her chin to her chest in resignation, realizing now that she'd been played.

"You're a bad girl," Leah told Tory when their kiss ended. "Sending that lamb for me to slaughter."

Tory grinned at Ryder. "Not me. It was Skyler's idea." She gave Leah another quick kiss. "But thanks for not doing permanent damage, babe."

"I am damaged." Ryder dramatically pressed her hands to her chest. "Shot down. Wounded."

Tory snorted. "I think your ego can stand a little deflating after your little rendezvous this morning in the airport storeroom."

Ryder grinned. "Claire was definitely a home run…this morning and all last week."

Jessica stood, with a little help from Skyler, and waved toward the table. "That sounds like a story we'd all like to hear, but let's sit down and eat while we talk." She rubbed her stomach. "This little girl is starving."

❖

"In a storeroom? With an FAA official? It's nice to know what our homeland-security dollars are paying for." Leah narrowed her eyes. "Maybe I should look into this more closely."

When Leah wasn't producing children's books with Bridgette, she contracted as an investigative reporter.

"Down, Sherlock," Tory said, laughing.

"It wasn't her fault," Ryder said smugly. "They only trained her to resist terrorists, not the patented Ryder charm." She grinned and wiggled her eyebrows to a chorus of groans from around the table.

Her earlier doubts about no longer fitting in with her friends evaporated as the evening progressed. She had missed the teasing and easy camaraderie. She had only temporary friendships with the grooms and riders who moved among the horse business like she did. And, unlike the polo or steeplechase crowd, the rodeo guys resented her intrusion into their men-only world, so the women she picked up for a fast fuck were mostly her only human contact.

It felt good to be here, almost like coming home to family. Correct that. Much better than being with her family. At least she felt genuine affection from her friends.

Skyler and Tory were the two people in the world who really knew her and would always have her back, even though she hadn't been much of a friend to them for a while. She felt a little ashamed about that, but they'd obviously been busy with their own personal pursuits.

Ryder instantly liked Jessica and Leah. They seemed to be perfect complements for her friends. Skyler was less angry with Jessica as her quiet, supportive anchor, and Tory relaxed and laughed a lot more with the sharp-witted, fiercely devoted Leah on her arm. She was happy for her friends, truly happy. And, perhaps, a little sad.

"I'm sorry. You caught me picking cotton." She realized everyone was looking at her for a response to a question she hadn't heard while she was deep in thought.

Skyler prompted her. "Tory wanted to know if you'd run into our notorious Alexandra while we were vetting horses this afternoon."

"Dunno. What's she look like?" Ryder sifted through her memory of the various people she'd met around the barns that afternoon.

"A redhead with big tits, the impulse control of a two-year-old, and the sex drive of a teenage boy," Leah said, her eyes flashing.

Jessica snorted. "Don't tell me she went after Tory, too. I had to threaten to call her husband if she didn't stop hitting on Skyler."

Leah glared at the memory. "She won't try it again."

"Wait. Who's Alexandra?"

Tory pointed her fork at Ryder. "Somebody you don't need to go looking for. That woman can smell new meat ten miles away. I'm betting she'll find you before the week's out."

Skyler laughed. "More like before the sun goes down tomorrow. Hey, we should set up a betting pool on how long it takes Ryder to nail Alex. Clint will want to get in the action, too," she said, referring to another trainer at the center.

Ryder threw a roll at Skyler's head. "Don't be crude. Can I help it if women enjoy me?" She ducked when the roll came flying back. "Besides, how do you know I'll even be interested?"

"You children stop playing with the food," Jessica said, taking a second roll from Skyler before she could launch it across the table, too.

"She's attractive, with no inhibitions and a husband to pay her bills. Exactly your type," Tory said, accepting a fist-bump from Skyler for being on the money.

"Maybe I want someone with a little more depth. What about the artist Jessica said couldn't make it tonight? Tell me about her."

Skyler nodded. "Looks like Amy Irving. You know, the actress?"

"Not your type, Ryder," Tory growled. "Leave it alone."

"I say turn the hound dog loose. Bridgette's a big girl. She doesn't need anybody to screen her dates." Leah threw her napkin on the table. "Jess, why don't you show me what you've done lately in the nursery? The testosterone in this room is stifling."

"Uh-oh. You lit the fuse on the firecracker for sure," Skyler said, as they watched Jessica and Leah go inside. "Looks like Leah's still touchy about the 'art lessons' you had before y'all got together. Glad I'm not going home with you."

"Shut up."

Ryder grinned at Tory's scowl. This was why she didn't do relationships. No strings meant no apologies. Obviously, Tory had something she'd have to smooth over later. "So, Tor, old buddy. Tell me about the artist."

Tory's gaze lingered a moment on the back door where Leah had gone, and then she shrugged and turned back to them. "Bridgette's cool. An amazing artist. Her stuff sells mostly out of a few galleries in New York and Boston. She also teaches at Earnhardt and illustrates a series of children's books for Leah on the side."

Ryder waved her hand to encourage more detail. "I want to hear about *your* art lessons." Judging by the flush creeping up Tory's cheeks, Bridgette definitely would be worth pursuit.

"Bridgette and I dated before Leah and I got together. We both knew it wasn't anything serious, so there were no hard feelings when I fell for Leah. We're all friends now."

"You fucked her, didn't you?" Ryder leaned over the table and grinned. "On a scale of one to ten, how hot is she?"

Tory glared at her. "Bridgette is one of the most mature, centered people I know. She'll never fall for your stupid pick-up lines."

"One to ten. How is she?"

"None of your business."

"Aw, come on, T. I know you want to tell me."

"You're such a dog." Tory stood and began stacking the plates and dishes to take them into the kitchen.

"So, what's your timetable?" Skyler asked, changing the subject. "You gonna relax with us for a while?"

Ryder shrugged. "One doc says three months. But the rodeo doc says they'll clear me in half that time if I promise to tuck and roll when I hop off, rather than landing on my feet for the crowd."

"There's no rush, Ryder. This is home as long as you need it. Unless you were planning to stay at the estate."

"No. I might go over to see what has to be done to sell it, but I don't want to stay there. I don't want to wear out my welcome here either."

"Not possible. We have four empty bedrooms upstairs, and, frankly, with the baby coming in a month, I can use the help. I've got a rider for the horses I'm training, but she's young. I need someone with experience looking over her shoulder while I'm busy. And when I have to be away for a show on Saturdays, I want to know someone else is here with Jess."

It was one small favor and Ryder owed Skyler many. She nodded. "Until my leg is healed enough to go back, I'll help any way I can." Except for the sponsor contracts she signed for the rodeo, that promise was as close to a commitment as she'd ever get.

Skyler looked relieved.

"Except I don't change diapers."

Skyler laughed. "You think I'd let you touch my kid? You'd probably turn diapering into a timed event."

Tory laughed, too, and gave Ryder a one-armed hug. "Good to have you home, Ryder. Now help me with these dishes so I can defuse my firecracker before I take her home."

Ryder grabbed some plates and hobbled after Tory. "I'll wash if you tell me…one to ten. I'll bet she's a ten, right? That's why Leah's still jealous."

Tory shook her head. "Do *not* ask that in front of Leah or I'll break your other leg."

The dishes done and the nursery tour over, the group drifted outside to say good night to Tory and Leah. Every time Leah turned her back, Ryder held up her fingers and silently mouthed the corresponding numbers, "One to ten?" She dropped her hands quickly when Leah turned to her.

"So, how long you here for?"

"A couple months. Three, tops. I can't stay out of the limelight too long or my sponsor gets antsy about the money they're still paying me."

Leah looked her over, as if evaluating her worth. "I've done a few free-lance articles for sports magazines. I could put out some feelers to see who might be interested in a piece about you while you're here to rehab. That is, if you're interested."

"Sure. That'd be great." Ryder hesitated. "Do I get to read it before you publish? I don't want to be part of a rant about the dangers of rodeo and how it should be banned as a sport."

"Absolutely not." Leah crossed her arms. "It will have to contain a paragraph or two of statistics on rodeo injuries, or I wouldn't be doing a good job. You'll just have to trust me that the rest will be a profile of you, not a diatribe on the rodeo business."

Tory's nod told Ryder that Leah's word was good.

"I can live with that."

"Okay. I'll let you know." Leah turned to slide her hand down Tory's chest and tuck her fingers into the waistband of her jeans. "Come on, stud, let's go home. All this talk about hitting on women has put me in the mood to remind you why you chose me." She winked at Ryder before releasing Tory and getting into the BMW.

Tory slapped Ryder on the back and hopped into her veterinary truck to follow, but stopped before the truck had rolled more that a few feet. She lowered the window and grinned.

"Nine, maybe nine and a half. Leah's the only ten I know."

CHAPTER FIVE

Bridgette cursed the unmanned reception desk in the lobby of the art building. Another victim of budget cuts, the receptionist had been fired and only volunteers now manned the desk—when they could find them.

The auction committee was scheduled to meet tomorrow, and she needed the brochure that listed the art displayed in the building's lobby and gallery. Maybe they couldn't sell those paintings, but they could begin by contacting the donors and asking if they would also contribute something else for the auction.

The third drawer she opened revealed a stack of the glossy trifolds. She took several for the committee and laid the rest on the desk for people to help themselves.

She glanced down the list of paintings. *They have an Eleanor White displayed here?* She chastised herself for never taking a thorough tour of the gallery before now. The paintings in the lobby were familiar enough, but she'd done little more than glance around the cavernous solarium where an impressive collection was displayed on a maze of eight-foot-tall panels, bathed in natural light.

She made her way slowly around the gallery, making notes of artist names and donor plaques. Some obviously could be contacted directly. Others would take some research to track down. There were few people in the gallery, mostly students she ignored as she moved through the exhibit. But something in the husky voice that drifted her way made her look up from taking notes.

"Of course it's art. It may be computer-generated, but the very concept began as a seed in the mind of the artist. I'm sure the artist started with a concept, then a vision. Bringing this to life may have been much more difficult than layering paint on a canvas."

Bridgette stepped around a panel to where two figures sat on a low bench, staring at the digital projection of a pink dogwood tree as it budded, bloomed, deflowered, grew leaves, swayed in the wind, drank rain droplets, withered and dropped its summer foliage, then held its spindly branches out to catch the winter snow before beginning the sequence all over again.

"It's a brilliant combination of display and performance art."

Ah. The husky voice again. She stared at the well-formed shoulders moving under a tight black T-shirt. The voice and the V-shaped body could easily be mistaken for that of a young man, but the slight flair of the hips in the low-slung jeans and the gesturing of the hands held a hint of femininity. Intrigued, Bridgette edged closer.

The thick, straight hair was cut in ragged lengths that barely brushed the shoulders in a style currently popular with the male art students. The arm that extended backward to brace the figure on the bench sported a black-dragon tattoo that peeked from under the short sleeve straining to contain a well-developed bicep. But the bare forearm was smooth and the hair on it fine, not coarse. The hand was long-fingered and, Bridgette decided, fine-boned enough to be female.

This person was deliciously androgynous and oddly familiar, but she met a lot of new people in her teaching job and was sure she would've remembered the large, black brace wrapped around the woman's left knee.

"Well, it is quite mesmerizing." The very elderly art patron chuckled and patted the arm of her much-younger companion. "And your enthusiasm for this piece is just as entertaining. However, I must be off. My grandson is probably waiting rather impatiently. I'm sure his class is over by now."

The younger person stood and helped the woman to her feet, and Bridgette decided the gentle outline of the cheek and full lips was definitely female, as was the lack of beard stubble. Perfect.

"Would you like me to walk with you to find your grandson?"

"Thank you, no. I may be old, but I'm still perfectly able to get around by myself." The old woman straightened as much as her bowed spine would allow. "At least I'm not using one of those yet," she said, pointing to the black cane still propped against the bench.

The younger woman's laugh came from deep in her chest, low and sexy. She retrieved the cane from where it rested and put her finger to her lips. "Don't tell anyone, but it's hollow. As soon as you leave, I'm going to cut that painting over there out of the frame, roll it up, and conceal it inside the cane. It should bring a nice price on the black market."

The elderly lady waved her hand dismissively. "Still a jokester, I see. I might have believed you, but I'm sure you have a dozen like them already." She turned toward the door. "Lovely to see you again, dear."

The old lady had barely left when Bridgette stepped forward. "Excuse me."

The woman turned, her amused dark eyes flicking over Bridgette. "Hello." A broad smile dimpled her tanned cheeks as they looked each other over for a few seconds. She tapped the cane against the bench. "It isn't really hollow, and even if it was, I don't think I could stuff an entire painting inside."

"It would have been interesting to watch you try, I'm sure."

Now that she was facing Bridgette, the woman's female attributes were obvious. Her height topped Bridgette's by a few inches, but small, well-rounded breasts softened her muscled upper body, and her narrow hips flared slightly from the trim waist.

"I actually wanted to see if you would be interested in a rather unusual opportunity."

The smile broadened to a grin. "I'm always interested in opportunities with attractive women."

Heat rose to Bridgette's cheeks, but she dipped her head in acknowledgement of the compliment. "Let's try this again." She extended her hand. "Hello. I'm Bridgette LeRoy. I teach art and body sculpture here."

The woman's grin grew wider. "Bridgette isn't a common name in these parts." The hand that grasped Bridgette's was rough but warm, and the lips that pressed against her knuckles soft. "Marc Ryder. Most people just call me Ryder."

Bridgette was amused by the gallant gesture. The woman looked more mature than the usual coed, but the college did have some older students enrolled. "Are you a student here, Ms. Ryder?"

"No, I'm not. I dropped by to talk to one of your professors, but his secretary said he was teaching a class so I wandered downstairs to peruse the gallery."

"You're an artist?" Bridgette let her eyes trail down Ryder's well-defined forearm to her long fingers. She turned over the hand that still held hers and examined the thick calluses. "Sculptor?"

The dark eyes twinkled. "Wrong again. I just appreciate beauty… in art and women."

Bridgette met her gaze. "Well, you're not bashful, are you? That's good, considering what I want to propose."

"My answer is yes."

Bridgette laughed. "I haven't explained anything yet."

"Will it injure me in any way?"

"Heavens no."

"Then my answer is yes." Ryder's hand tightened around hers. "But perhaps we could discuss the details over dinner."

"You said you were here to see someone."

Ryder waved her hand dismissively. "Nothing is more important than having dinner with a beautiful woman."

She hesitated. Ryder was athletic, confident, and oozing sexuality—certainly the androgynous type she found attractive. Besides, serial killers were almost always men. What could it hurt to have dinner? She eyed Ryder's strong body. She certainly wasn't opposed to a little adventure afterward either.

"How to you feel about sushi?"

"Love it."

She glanced at the brace on Ryder's left knee. "I'll drive."

Ryder grinned. "I love a woman who takes charge."

❖

It was still early and the restaurant was relatively empty, so it only took a few minutes to be seated and place their order.

Acutely aware of Bridgette continually checking out her physique, Ryder couldn't believe her luck. How many artists named Bridgette lived in Cherokee Falls? This woman had to be Tory's nine-and-a-half, and Ryder intended to confirm it.

"So, what I wanted to propose to you—"

Ryder held up her hand. "A woman likes to be wined and dined before a proposal."

Truth was, Ryder wanted to wine and dine Bridgette. She intended to savor this beautiful, soft-voiced woman sitting across the table from her.

Bridgette's expression was smug. "You've already said yes. I was just going to fill in the details."

"There's so much I'd like to know before we get to that. I grew up around here and I'm pretty sure you didn't. Tell me about yourself. Where did you grow up?"

"Everywhere. Mostly the northeast when we were in the country. My father was a professor of political science. He job-hopped a lot, teaching at universities on the East Coast and managing a political campaign every now and then. More than once, he accepted a foreign-ambassador position when his candidate held the seat of power."

"A well-traveled woman. What brought you to Cherokee Falls?"

"My cousin had a hand in it." Bridgette dropped her gaze, her fingers worrying with her napkin. "I was sort of at loose ends." Her smile was a bit forced when she looked up. "So, my cousin Cheryl convinced me to apply for the artist-in-residence position here. The college may be small, but it's well-known in some key art circles."

They paused while the waitress set a sushi platter between them and poured the wine Ryder had ordered. Recognizing Bridgette's discomfort with her past, she steered the conversation toward preferences in art, music, books, and movies as they ate. But each time Bridgette asked about her career or friends in Cherokee Falls, she neatly deflected the questions and sent the conversation in a different direction. She didn't want to chance Bridgette connecting her to stories Skyler or Tory might have told about her.

"May I inquire about who you wanted to see at the art school today?" Bridgette asked.

"Jonathan Frank is a family friend. I wanted to get some guidance from him on what to do with some things from my grandmother's estate."

"Your grandmother?"

"She died a few years ago and I'm her sole heir. I'm just getting around to deciding what to do with her house and the stuff still in it."

"I'm so sorry for your loss."

Ryder shrugged. "We weren't that close." Time to change the subject. "I didn't see a Bridgette LeRoy in the gallery. Do you paint under an alias?"

"No." Bridgette chewed for a moment and pushed the food around on her plate. "The department chairman has been pressuring me to contribute something, but, well, I just haven't yet."

"I'm disappointed. Isn't there somewhere I can see your work?"

"I have some paintings and a sculpture or two in galleries in New York and Boston."

Bridgette took a sip of her wine, and Ryder captured her hand when she put her glass down.

"You sculpt, too?" She turned Bridgette's hand over and lightly traced the soft palm with her fingertips, pleased at the faint tremble she evoked. "I wouldn't have guessed. No calluses."

"I sculpt in clay, not stone."

"Ah, that explains it." She caressed Bridgette's palm once more before releasing her, pleased when Bridgette picked up her wineglass and gulped down a large swallow. She suspected it wasn't just the alcohol coloring Bridgette's cheeks.

"If you're really interested, I can write the names of the galleries down for you. They both post their offerings on their Web sites."

"I'd like that, but the Internet is so impersonal. Every artist I've known has a studio filled with their work. I was hoping for a personal showing."

"I'm not sure I want to get personal with someone I know nothing about. What do you do for a living?"

"I work in the sports field."

"I don't really follow sports."

"Then I won't bore you with the details."

Ryder noticed that Bridgette gravitated toward the spicy tuna, so she had taken only one piece and left the rest of it for Bridgette. She snagged the last piece with her chopsticks and held it up. She watched Bridgette hesitate, then take it gently on her tongue and into her mouth to chew slowly. When Ryder looked up, a blazing gaze captured her.

They both smiled, acknowledging the mutual seduction. If they didn't get out of that restaurant soon, the heat between them would cook every piece of sushi in the place.

"My personal studio is at my loft," Bridgette said.

"If that's an invitation, I accept." Ryder tossed enough money on the table for the meal and a generous tip, then slid out of the booth and held out her hand to assist Bridgette. "I've always found art to be very…inspiring."

Chapter Six

Their journey to the loft was one long, hot tease. During their walk to the car, Bridgette linked her arm in Ryder's, taking every opportunity to brush her tantalizingly erect nipple against Ryder's bicep as they flirted. By the time they had reached the parking lot, Ryder had slipped her arm around Bridgette's waist and drifted her hand down to palm Bridgette's firm ass. She teased back, pressing Ryder against the car as she unlocked it, then stepping away just as their lips were a hairbreadth from their first kiss. Once in the car, Ryder took her hand and pressed it against her hard thigh. She retaliated by inching her hand upward until her pinkie barely touched the damp heat of Ryder's crotch. She smiled when Ryder groaned under her breath.

She jogged to her second-floor loft while Ryder's cane thumped noisily along the stairs behind her. Disengaging the lock, she grabbed fistfuls of Ryder's T-shirt and yanked her inside. As they stood breast to breast, Ryder's breath was hot on her face, her whisky eyes smoldering. She grazed her lips against Ryder's, dodging her head away as Ryder's mouth chased hers.

"I thought you wanted a personal tour of my studio."

Ryder abandoned pursuit of her lips and sucked the pulse throbbing at the base of her neck, then licked upward. "I'd like to get to know the artist first."

Her hips jerked when Ryder's teeth nipped at her sensitive earlobe. She tore Ryder's shirt from her jeans and raked her fingernails across her abdomen.

Ryder growled. She threw her cane to the floor, shoved the door closed, and whirled them around to pin her against it. The heavy oak was hard against her back. Ryder's mouth was demanding, her tongue searching. She tasted of the woody bouquet from the wine they'd had with dinner. She skated her hand up to Ryder's small breast and twisted the nipple hard. Ryder's hips bucked against hers, her thigh rolling against Bridgette's crotch. Sweet Jesus.

Bridgette felt like she was on a runaway horse, galloping toward a thousand-foot drop. No woman had ever gotten her this hot, this fast. Slow down. She needed to slow down. She shoved Ryder away and they stood panting, staring at each other.

"About that proposal."

Confusion flashed across Ryder's face, and then she narrowed her eyes and a slow smile dimpled one cheek. "I'm up for anything you are as long as it's not too kinky."

"I want you to pose for my art class."

Confusion flickered again.

"Now?"

"Next week."

"Fine. I said I'd do it." Ryder reached for her.

"Nude."

Ryder froze, then dropped her hands and laughed. "You thought you'd get me all worked up so I'd agree to anything you wanted?"

She stepped close again and traced her finger along Ryder's cheek. "You've already said yes. Remember?"

"So?"

She trailed her finger down Ryder's neck to tug at the collar of her shirt. "So, I want a," she moved her finger lower to circle hard nipples straining against the cotton fabric, "preview of my model."

Ryder stepped close to whisper in her ear. "I'll show you mine if you'll show me yours."

She shivered but again pushed Ryder gently away. "We'll get to me later."

Ryder's grin was cocky. She jerked her shirt over her head in one quick motion. The tight material had done little to hide the well-defined shoulders and arms, but her breath hitched at the sight of Ryder's small, soft breasts and carved abdomen. Her fingers itched to touch, but she drew in a deep breath and forced herself to focus with her artist's eye instead of the throbbing between her legs.

She pointed to the knee brace wrapped over Ryder's jeans. "Can you take that off?"

Ryder didn't answer but snatched the Velcro straps open and tossed the brace to the floor. While her hands had worked quickly on the brace, they moved slowly over the buttons of her fly. The loose jeans dropped to the floor, revealing skin-hugging, low-cut black boy shorts and thick, firm thighs. Bridgette barely had time to register the roadwork of red scars along her left leg before Ryder turned away.

Sinewy lines moved smoothly under the flawless skin of her back as she hooked her thumbs under the Lycra material and slowly drew it down to reveal a tight, compact butt. Deep clefts on the sides of the rounded cheeks flexed as she shifted her weight.

Bridgette circled, evaluating the boi-god, warrior-goddess physique. Well-defined and nicely muscled, but not too bulky. From the back, a careless eye would see a man. A careful eye would notice the faint flair of the hip, the lack of masculine hair, and the softer grain of the skin.

"Perfect," she murmured to herself.

"Thank you."

Lost in her observations, she jerked her gaze back to Ryder's face after the husky voice startled her. Her expression had gone from smug to curious.

She should explain. "I want my students to recognize the subtle indicators of gender when they paint and sculpt." She continued to circle, taking careful note, while Ryder stood as still as chiseled stone and let her look. "Our perceptions in general are shaped mostly by the dominant sex, by men. Conventional attitudes are that women are poorly muscled and have an hourglass shape."

"I'm often mistaken for a man."

"That's why I approached you in the gallery."

"I'm crushed. I thought maybe you were hot for me."

She ignored the implied question for now. "From this view, you might be mistaken for a male. But an artist should be able to see the female."

Ryder crossed her arms over her chest, flexing her back into a wide *V*-shape. Bridgette smoothed her fingers along the overly developed trapezius and latissimus dorsi above and below the shoulder blade. "These might be mistaken for masculine but," she ran her hand down the trenched center of Ryder's back, pleased at the faint shudder she felt, "the lumbar curve of your spine is definitely female. Women are more sway-backed than men, tilting their pelvis backward."

In front of Ryder again, she moved her hands along the collarbone and over the firm deltoids of the shoulders. "Your shoulders are actually probably no wider than mine, even though the larger muscles make them seem broader." She squeezed the hard biceps, then scooped Ryder's hands into hers. "Interesting."

"Something wrong with my hands?"

She moved them up and matched them with hers, palm to palm. Ryder's hands were wider, hers longer. "On the majority of women, the index finger and the ring finger are usually the same length...like mine. Men generally have a shorter index finger...like yours."

She entwined their fingers and squeezed briefly before dropping her hands to Ryder's hips. "Even though you have very narrow hips for a woman, the hipbone still flairs slightly." She crouched and squeezed Ryder's thick quads. "Because a woman has a wider pelvis, her femurs are angled inward, shaping their legs into a slight X-shape."

Ryder widened her stance a little. Eye-level with the short, dark curls, she breathed in the musky scent of Ryder's arousal and looked up. Her eyes dark as chocolate and hungry, Ryder held out her hand and she took it as she stood.

"My turn," Ryder said. "You left a few things out."

Ryder held her gaze and worked her silk blouse open, button by button, then dropped it to the hardwood floor.

"A woman's skin is like satin." Ryder touched her cheek with the backs of her fingers.

Ryder released the front clasp of her bra and laid her cheek against Bridgette's chest. "Her breasts like the finest silk pillows."

Sliding behind her, Ryder reached around to pop the button on her leg-hugging jeans and lowered the zipper. She could feel the hard points of Ryder's nipples against her shoulders and the calluses of her hands as they slid under the material to push it down.

"A woman's body has curves like a mountain road, rather than sharp turns."

Ryder appeared to have no trouble bearing weight on her healing leg, but difficulty bending it, so she helped by toeing off her ankle-high boots and bending to wiggle out of her jeans. She had barely straightened when Ryder molded to her back and held her firmly.

"But I don't need to see to know male from female."

Her flesh tingled as Ryder nuzzled her neck and inhaled deeply. "A woman smells of lilacs," she gasped when Ryder cupped her sex, then lifted her glistening fingers to her nose, "and musk."

Ryder's mouth was on her neck now. "A woman tastes both sweet—"

She held her breath and watched out of the corner of her eye as Ryder sucked on the fingers she'd just sniffed.

Ryder groaned and she rubbed her hips against Bridgette's ass. "—and salty."

The last words, a hoarse rasp, flooded her crotch and dripped down her thighs. Her legs shook with her need to come. She wheeled to grasp Ryder behind her neck and, when their mouths met in a frantic devouring feast, she realized Ryder's need burned as hot and bright as hers.

Ryder's hands were on her buttocks, massaging and lifting her. She wrapped her legs around the trim waist and they both moaned as she rubbed her slick clit against Ryder's belly. She tightened her legs without breaking their kiss, and Ryder carried her toward the only interior doorway in the open loft.

The red silk sheets were a rumpled pool on the king-sized bed. She bounced slightly when Ryder dropped her onto the mattress, finally breaking their kiss. Ryder's eyes bored into hers, dark and wild. Her chest was flushed, her nipples stiff as she climbed onto the bed and hovered over her.

"Damn, you're gorgeous," Ryder said. "I hope you've got all night, because I've got a long list I want to check off with you."

"Good." She was a bit out of breath. "I was afraid you were one of those one-and-done kind of women."

Ryder threw her head back and laughed. "Hardly. When I get done with you, beautiful, you're gonna know what it means to be rode hard and put up wet."

Before she could answer, Ryder sucked her breast into her hot mouth. Her hips jerked and her thighs fell open as a hard nip sent a wave of pleasure all the way to her toes. Ryder took the opening and moved between her legs, holding her thighs apart with her weight.

"I love a woman who likes it a little rough," she said.

She grabbed a fistful of Ryder's dark hair and yanked her down for another forceful kiss. Their tongues battled. She opened her legs wider and dug her fingernails into Ryder's ass. Ryder bucked, rubbing their clits together, and they growled into each other's mouths as they began a furious hump. They were both so wet, so hot.

The pressure gliding against her clit was too much, and she whimpered as her orgasm gathered in her belly. She broke their kiss and screamed at the ceiling as it swarmed through, convulsing her body. A second later, Ryder's body went rigid and she joined her with a muffled groan.

Her legs were still trembling from the aftershocks when Ryder slithered down and slipped her shoulders under her thighs. She sucked in her breath when Ryder opened her with her fingers and greedily bathed her with her tongue.

God, she was good. The talented mouth probed and swirled and lapped and probed until she began to wonder if Ryder was a medical freak with two tongues, at least one of them unnaturally long. Her heart hadn't slowed from her first climax when the second orgasm flashed through her.

This time, when the spots before her eyes cleared, she was cradled against Ryder's soft breast and warm hands stroked her back.

"Wow."

"You okay? I think you may have left me for a minute."

"Wow." She wasn't sure, but she thought maybe she did black out for a second or two.

Ryder chuckled. "We must have killed some brain cells. I know you definitely short-circuited mine, and you seem to be reduced to a one-word vocabulary."

She rubbed her cheek against Ryder's still-hard nipple. She was surprised that she felt energized rather than depleted.

"Still want to see my studio?"

"Do we have to get dressed?"

"Not unless you're cold-natured or modest."

"What do you think?"

Bridgette kissed her, tasting herself on Ryder's lips before pushing inside to languidly roll their tongues together, then ending it with one last brush of their lips. She studied Ryder's oval-shaped face and strong jaw. She hadn't noticed before how long and thick her dark lashes were.

"I think you're hot-blooded and completely without modesty," she said. "Why haven't I met you before now?"

"Karma? Fate? Just plain bad luck?"

"You didn't just get out of prison, did you?"

Ryder laughed. "No. I've never even spent a night in jail." She looked thoughtful. "No, wait. That's not true. There was that one night in Texas. But that wasn't my fault. The woman didn't tell me she was married and that her husband's father was the county sheriff."

She shook her head and climbed out of the bed. "Should I get your cane?"

"Nah. I don't use the cane or the brace anymore around the house, unless I have to tackle steps."

However, she didn't miss the care Ryder took to stand gradually and the effort to hide her limp as they walked through the loft to her studio space behind the massive stone fireplace.

The room was filled with half-finished canvases, some sitting on easels and others stacked in the corner. Sketches were pinned to the wall around a tilted art table littered with more drawings. The fore part of a horse was emerging from a large block of clay on small, elevated table in the center of the room.

Bridgette was suddenly uncomfortable, watching Ryder carefully examine each painting. She glanced at her several times as she rounded the room. Did she notice that nothing was finished? Ryder touched the clay sculpture, then looked up, seeming puzzled.

"Your clay is dry. You don't intend to finish this?" Ryder looked at the sketches laid out on the floor around the sculpture. "The sketches are great."

Bridgette shrugged. "I got sidetracked onto another project and sort of lost interest in that. I've been meaning to throw it out."

Ryder frowned, her brow furrowed, but didn't reply as she continued around the room. She seemed to know more than the average person about art.

"You haven't really told me what you do for a living. All you said was it involved sports. Are you a sports photographer or artist? You seem to have a good eye for it."

"No. I just enjoy art." She walked over to the sketching desk and picked up a copy of *Sure and the Groundhog.* "Doing a little light reading?"

She smiled. "A little light drawing. That's the third in a series of children's books that I illustrate for a writer friend. I enjoy doing it, and I've been surprised at how much money you can make from successful children's literature."

Ryder thumbed through the pages. "This is really cute. You like kids?"

"I do, but don't plan to have any. I enjoy my cousin's children, and I have some friends about to have their first baby. They own an equestrian training center just outside town."

"You like horses?"

"They're beautiful animals. I've been thinking about taking a few riding lessons to see if I like it."

Ryder nodded and turned to a large, unopened crate in the far corner of the room.

"What's in this?"

She frowned. It hadn't bothered her at all that they were prowling her studio in the nude, but seeing Ryder examine the crate made her feel suddenly exposed.

"Are you thirsty? I am." She walked quickly back to the main part of the loft and pulled two bottles of water from the refrigerator. She downed half a bottle, then grabbed a corkscrew and a black-raspberry merlot from her wine rack.

Ryder limped around the fireplace, waving a sketchpad. "You weren't going to show me this, were you?"

"Drink this." She thrust the second bottle of water at Ryder, then took the pad and laid it on the counter. She uncorked the wine and poured two glasses.

Ryder emptied her bottle of water in one long drink and picked up the sketchpad again and the wine she offered, sipping as she paged through slowly. The figures were faceless outlines, but all female, either erotically or romantically entwined. She gulped down her wine and refilled the glass as she watched Ryder's face.

"This is definitely not for a children's book," Ryder murmured, her gaze fixed on a sketch of two women. The reclining figure's head was thrown back, wavy tresses draped over her shoulders, while the other figure, barely more than an outline, kneeled with her hand between the first figure's legs.

Ryder flipped to the next drawing and licked her lips. "Shit."

Was it the picture or the wine that was flushing Ryder's chest and cheeks? It pleased her that her drawings aroused Ryder. She moved to rub her breasts against Ryder's bare back and whisper in her ear. "That's one of my favorites."

Ryder gulped down the rest of her wine, then returned her gaze to the sketch. The long-haired figure was kneeling, adjusting the straps of a dildo harness around the hips of a standing figure.

"Why don't they have faces?"

She brushed her fingers down Ryder's ribs, scraping her nails across the ridges that twitched under her touch.

"I dream about them, but I can never see their faces. Still, they inspire me." She moved her hand downward to comb her fingers through Ryder's stiff curls. She was wet. "Apparently, I'm not the only one feeling inspired."

She released Ryder and emptied the last of the wine into their glasses. Then she took her glass and sauntered back to the bedroom, leaving Ryder to follow.

She barely had time to put her glass down and sit on the bed when Ryder was standing before her. "In the drawer," she said, indicating the nightstand.

Ryder stepped into the dark leather harness and efficiently tightened it around her slim hips. Her gaze was a keen razor as she silently handed over a small bottle. She spread the lubricant along the flesh-colored dildo, pleased when Ryder's hips jerked as she pumped it several times. She lay back across the bed and opened her legs.

Ryder's body was hot as she covered her, the cock slick between their bellies. Their kiss was slow and deep and thorough. She hummed at the feel of Ryder's mouth sucking her throbbing pulse, then moaned as Ryder's callused hand massaged her breast while her teeth found the nipple of her other.

Sharp pleasure pulsed from her breasts to her clit. She opened wider and pulled her knees up. She was ready. She was dripping. She needed Ryder to fill her, to take her.

Ryder's warm hand left her breast, and the head of the dildo pressed against her entrance.

"Yes," she hissed. "Please, yes."

She pressed her heels against Ryder's ass. She was so open, so slick, that she took the thick cock easily. They both groaned. Ryder kissed her again then rose to rest her weight on her elbows and her good knee. She stared down at her, her eyes bright as she began a slow pump of her hips.

Good. It felt so good. She closed her eyes as Ryder gave two short pumps, scraping the cock's head against the spot that sent waves of pleasure down her legs and into her belly. The next stroke pushed deep to fill her completely. A swirl of her hips brushed the leather harness against her swollen clit.

"Sweet mother. You're good with that."

Ryder slipped her forearms under her back to pull her closer and tease her breast with her tongue as she thrust, settling into a steady pace that lifted her to the breath-stealing, toe-curling edge of ecstasy and held her there.

"I should be," Ryder mumbled against the nipple in her mouth. "I'm a professional rider."

CHAPTER SEVEN

S ure, I know a few artists who may be willing to donate something to your auction. E-mail me the details and I'll make a few phone calls."

"Thanks, Lydia. You're a lifesaver. I'm not sure how I got roped into this." Bridgette cradled the phone against her ear with her shoulder so her hands were free to mix the paints she had squirted onto a fresh palette.

"Do you want me to send something of yours back for the auction?"

"I was thinking I might paint something new, but what do you have left?"

The long, uncomfortable silence was followed by a deep sigh. "All of it."

She laid her mixing brush down and climbed onto the tall swivel chair at her sketching table. "You haven't sold one thing?"

"I'd have sent a check if I had. You know that."

She did know it. But she had chosen not to think about the absence of a check from Lydia's galleries or a call begging her to send more of her work. She frowned and rubbed at her forehead as if she could massage that nagging reality back behind the door she kept tightly closed.

"You need to get out of that place, Bridge. You haven't painted a single thing I can sell since you moved there."

"I've found peace here, Lydia."

"You've lost passion. It shows in your art. That's why I can't sell it. Pretty pictures only sell at street fairs. My patrons know the difference."

Her laugh was bitter. "Ouch. Tell me what you really think."

"Send me the crate in your studio. You haven't even opened it, have you?"

She didn't answer.

"It's your best work and you know it."

Silence.

Lydia's voice softened. "Stephan wouldn't want this. He wouldn't want you to hide and bottle up your talent. He loved you too much."

"Stephan only loved himself and the next thrill he could find."

"You know that's not fair."

She closed her eyes against the pain that threatened to split her chest. She wouldn't cry. "I can't," she whispered. "I can't open that crate and I can't sell what's in it either. It still hurts too much."

"Oh, honey. Come up for a visit. We'll go out, see a show, do something fun."

She took a deep breath. "Okay. Maybe I will. But not until after the auction. I won't have time before then."

"I'm going to hold you to that. In the meantime, find something hot to fuck. That is, if they have any hot bootie down there in the boonies."

"Oh, trust me, we don't have a shortage of hot women here. Maybe you should come down for the auction and see for yourself."

"Maybe I will, darling. I'll be in touch. Ciao."

"Bye, Lydia."

She ended the call, surprised that a tingling in her belly had replaced the pain in her chest. New York lesbians had nothing on the local talent in Cherokee Falls. It had been two days and she still was a tad sore from the all-night marathon of screaming orgasms with Ryder. Two days since she'd awakened to find a note tented on the pillow next to hers.

Early morning physical therapy appointment. You were so beautiful and sleeping so soundly, I didn't want to wake you. You are amazing. See you in art class. Ryder

She wasn't sure Ryder would really show up because she hadn't even told her when and where. But spending that one night with Ryder had her mixing paint for the first time in months. She picked up her palette and stood in front of the blank, white canvas. The images flashing through her mind definitely would have to be sold in New York, not locally. She turned the canvas to a horizontal position and began to paint.

Several hours later, the outline of two women on a bed was taking shape, bathed in the warm, muted light of a bedside lamp, their legs entwined. One figure lay with her back arched and breasts offered up to the second, who was propped on one elbow as she hovered over the reclining woman. Her mouth was on the first woman's breast, her hand delving between her lover's legs.

She painted quickly. It was good. She knew it was good because of the dampness of her panties. The scene was crystal clear in her head and flowing freely onto the canvas. She paused her work on the figures to fill in the satin sheets that draped the bed.

After she squeezed small amounts of blue, green, and burnt umber on a clean corner of her palette, she frowned. She must have used up her tube of cadmium red. She put her brush down and retrieved a fresh one from her supply cabinet. Her gaze returned to the figures as she squirted out a generous amount from the fresh tube, the thoughts jumping forward to the flesh colors she would mix next. She closed her eyes and became the figure lying on her back with Ryder hovering over her—tanned face, flushed chest, and dark nipples.

First, the sheets.

She looked down to mix the colors and her heart stuttered.

Red, crimson red. She was suddenly on that balcony in Pamplona, Spain.

Men in white clothing are wearing vivid red sashes tied around their waists. Running. The street is filled with running men. Onlookers are hanging out of open windows and cheering from balconies that look down on the narrow avenue. The din rises as dark, hulking shapes gallop after the scrambling runners. The bulls swing their massive horns, goring each other and the men they overtake. Bodies are tossed like rag dolls into the air while others are trampled underfoot.

Screams join the crowd's frenzied cheering as runners scale barriers, gutters, anything to escape the carnage. Blood, fresh and bright, is everywhere as the seething mass of bulls and men moves to the next block.

They are gone, but a blond-haired figure remains splayed in the street, unmoving below her. Blood, crimson blood pools around it. She is numb. No. That's not him. That's not HIM. Stephan!

Her paintbrush and palette clattered to the floor as she sank to her knees, sobbing. She hadn't relived that nightmare in years. Why had her torment returned? Why now?

❖

"So, why rodeo?"

Ryder grinned and settled back into an overstuffed leather chair in the den at Skyler and Jessica's house. "I feel sexy when I put on my chaps."

"I'm going to quote you on that, but you need to dig a little deeper if this interview's going to be worth publishing," Leah said, tapping her fingers impatiently against her laptop.

"You want me to expose myself? How about if I strip naked to set the mood?"

"Believe it or not, that's not the strangest suggestion I've had from someone I've interviewed." Leah's gaze met hers. "So, if it helps you, go right ahead. It won't change the questions I'm going to ask. In fact, I could snap a photo or two of the scars on your leg."

Leah's message was loud and clear. This was business. When Ryder was nervous, flirting was her fallback because it usually put her in control. And Leah made her nervous.

She was very attractive, with a mesmerizing syrupy accent. No wonder Tory had fallen in love with her. Her five-five height was fairly average for a woman, but she was so fine-boned that she appeared physically small. Small, but not fragile. When Leah walked into the room, she wielded a sharp intelligence and carried an alpha-sized attitude that made people step back. Ryder wasn't accustomed to someone who was so direct, so unaffected by her charm.

Leah seemed to read her discomfort and softened a bit. "Just be yourself, Ryder. That's how you prefer to be addressed, right?"

She shifted uncomfortably but dropped the flirty act. "Yeah. That's what my friends call me."

Leah waited for more, and she finally nodded.

"Okay. My friends all started calling me by my last name when I was a teenager because all I wanted to do was be a professional rider, from the first time I climbed up on a horse. It just kinda stuck and I got used to it." And using her last name helped her keep people at a safe distance. Even her best friends.

"What do your parents call you?"

She frowned. "That subject is off-limits. My parents dumped me on my grandmother when I was six and pretty much walked out of my life."

"How about I just say your grandmother raised you?"

"Good enough."

"How did you start riding horses? Or more specifically, what was your first experience with a horse?"

"Well, I guess I was sort of a handful when I hit my teen years. My grandmother was friends with Leigh Parker, who started the Young Equestrian Program for kids who needed to focus their energy on something positive. So, one day when she was trying to paint and I was underfoot—"

"Painting? Are we talking about a picture or a room?"

"My grandmother, Eleanor White, was an artist."

"I'm not big into art, but I've heard the name." Leah typed it into her notes. "I'll look her up later, and I may have a few more questions after I do that."

"That's fine."

"So, tell me about your first time on a horse."

She was warmed by the memory. "Eleanor was at her wits' end with me, so she put me in the car and we drove over here to the equestrian center."

"Back up. What exactly were you doing that was irritating your grandmother?"

"The usual teen stuff—blasting rock music over my stereo, slamming doors, smoking pot in my bedroom and not even trying to hide it." She grinned at Leah. "I think she was mostly pissed that I'd found her stash and helped myself."

"I might leave that part out. We wouldn't want to sic the cops on Grandma."

She shrugged. "Eleanor died about five years ago. It'd be hard to arrest her now."

Leah looked up from taking notes and raised an eyebrow, but she held her gaze in challenge. What was Leah expecting? Tears for the woman who couldn't bring herself to comfort a child crying for her absent parents?

"What happened when she brought you here?"

"When we got here, Leigh was at the outdoor ring, watching her daughter, Kate, work a new stallion. Kate was pretty much running the kids' program by then, so Leigh waved her over to get in on the discussion about what to do with me." Ryder chuckled. "I was thirteen and—"

"Trouble with a capital *T*." Tory stood in the doorway, smiling at Leah. "Sorry, babe. I was just here to check a few mares that are pregnant and saw your car. I didn't mean to interrupt. I forgot you were doing the interview."

"Maybe you should tell this part," Ryder said.

Leah held out her hand to beckon Tory over. "You were there?"

Tory entwined her fingers with Leah's and bent down for a quick kiss. "Yep. Skyler and I both were. We were watching Kate ride Dante for the first time."

"Every good profile requires input from people who know the subject. Why don't you join us for a few minutes?"

She shrugged again and nodded her consent when Tory looked at her to confirm she didn't mind.

"Ryder, why don't you start?" Leah, her hands poised over her laptop keyboard, scooted over to allow Tory to sit next to her on the sofa.

"Well, Eleanor was talking the ears off Kate and Leigh about her problems with me, so I wandered over to Sky and Tory. They were looking all important and full of themselves because Kate had handed the stallion over to them to watch while she talked."

Tory cut in. "You were the one trying to look all tough and full of yourself."

She laughed. "Sky and Tory were both sixteen, and Sky was dressed in riding breeches and knee-high boots that I thought were really cool. So, yeah, I was trying to impress the older kids."

Tory said, "She sauntered over and said, 'Nice horse.' Skyler always had a chip on her shoulder about the rich kids who owned horses at the center because most of them looked down on the trouble-making kids in Kate's program. And she hadn't missed that Ryder and Eleanor had driven up in a Mercedes, so—"

"So Tory jumped in before Sky could be a smart-ass and said, 'You ride?'" Ryder smiled, and Tory grinned back at her as they relived the scene together. "I said, 'No, but how hard can it be?'"

"You were such a punk," Tory said. "Skyler kinda snorted and says, 'A lot harder than you think, kid.'"

"I, of course, took that as sort of a dare. I didn't like being called *kid.*"

"Then Ryder says to Skyler, 'So you ride him?'"

"You two were so easy to play."

"Says you."

"It's the truth."

"Okay, children, focus for me."

Ryder returned to the story. "Skyler puffs up and says, 'Not yet, but I'll ride this big guy as soon as Kate says it's okay.' I couldn't resist yanking her chain, so I said, 'You think he's big? I've seen bigger horses.'"

Tory reached over and lightly slapped her on the back of the head. "It was just the first time this instigator got us all in trouble by taunting Sky into doing something she shouldn't."

"Anyway, Sky says, 'You'd probably wet your pants if I put you up in that saddle.' I said, 'Try me.'"

"Next thing I know, Skyler hands the reins to me and boosts this idiot into the saddle," Tory said. "I'll never forget her grinning down at us, grabbing a handful of mane, and saying 'Tallyho' right before she kicks that stallion hard in the sides and the reins jerk right out of my hands."

"Did you fall off?"

Tory answered for her. "Hell, no. The reins were dragging and the leathers were too long for her to get her feet in the stirrups, but she hunched over Dante's neck and hung on to his mane for dear life."

Ryder chuckled. "Sky was yelling her head off and Kate came running. It spooked the horse so bad, next thing I knew, he was sailing over the railing and we were headed down the driveway."

"Skyler ran across the road to the indoor ring where some kids were in the middle of a lesson," Tory said. "She snatched one of them off a horse, mounted up, and went chasing after her."

"Actually, I was kind of glad to see Sky show up, because I didn't have a clue how I was going to stop that stallion."

"I can imagine what she must have said when she caught you," Leah muttered as she typed.

"The weird thing was she didn't say anything at first. She just grabbed the stallion's reins and slowed us to a walk, then headed back." Ryder ducked her head, surprised that the memory choked her throat and made her eyes tear. "We were halfway back before—"

"Before I turned to her and said, 'You've got the biggest balls I've ever seen on a girl.'"

Now, Skyler stood in the doorway, and Ryder wondered if her two friends had appeared because they were curious or because they were being protective big sisters. She voted for the latter.

"Then she asked if I was going to board a horse and take lessons here. I told her, 'I guess that's up to Ms. Parker. I think Eleanor is dumping me out here so she doesn't have to deal with me anymore.'"

Skyler nodded. "That told me she was going to be one of Kate's kids like the rest of us, not one of those rich snots who always blamed their horses instead of their lousy riding when they didn't win ribbons."

"Still, I know you must have chewed her out for taking off on that stallion," Leah said to Skyler.

"Nope. I told her the chewing out she'd get from Kate would be a lot worse than anything I could come up with."

Ryder nodded. "Then she told me not to worry about it. Just keep my mouth shut until she was done, then promise I wouldn't do it again. She said Kate never stayed mad, and she was right."

Leah typed another minute, then looked up at Skyler and Tory. "This is good stuff, you guys, and I'm glad you popped in, but I need to finish the interview with Ryder alone."

Tory stood. "Okay. We get the message. Come on, Sky, I need to go over the foaling charts on the mares I just checked." She gave Leah another quick kiss and the two of them disappeared down the hallway to the farm office.

"Your background is—" Leah checked her notes. "Your background is dressage, eventing, polo and steeplechase racing in Europe. Those are really expensive sports, and people who participate aren't exactly middle class. When you switched to rodeo and the tobacco-spitting crowd, did you find it difficult to fit in?"

Ryder laughed. "Some of that crowd may have a chaw in their cheeks, but a lot of them aren't exactly middle class either. There's still big money behind it. It's just a different culture. Besides, I'm not there to fit in. I'm there to be noticed." The words were out of her mouth before she had time to evaluate them.

"Like the kind of notice you get from stealing a stallion when you're a kid?"

"I meant that I have to stand out enough to attract sponsors and fans."

"And you *have* been successful at attracting several big sponsors. Was that hard?"

"Not really. They back the riders they think will get their brand in front of the public the most. I do that."

"You have that many fans?"

"Some people are there cheering for me. But probably ten times as many are watching because they're waiting for the woman to get her butt kicked by a pissed-off bull. My sponsors don't care why they're watching, just that eight thousand people are in their seats with their eyes glued to the chute where I'll pop out wearing a shirt with their logo on it."

They talked for several minutes about the protective gear she used, and then Leah returned again to the big question.

"Why ride broncs and bulls?"

Ryder realized that was the gold nugget Leah was digging for to up the article's ante. She wasn't sure she could give it up, though, because even she hadn't been able to put her hands on it.

"I don't know. Maybe because they said I couldn't."

"So, you're out to prove women can do it, too?"

"No. I don't think I want to carry the weight of my entire gender on my shoulders. This is just about Marc Ryder. It's just about me and the thrill I get from doing it."

CHAPTER EIGHT

Ryder scanned the area as she parked the truck Skyler had loaned her. Dusk had settled in, but racks of overhead lights illuminated three ball fields still teeming with players. Not much had changed. New paint brightened the cinderblock dugouts and small building that housed restrooms and a concession stand, but the sponsors advertised on the uniforms and many of the players on the fields were familiar.

She grimaced when she dropped to the ground from the tall dually truck, taking most of her weight on her right leg. She'd been paying for her romp with Bridgette, but, damn, it was worth every ice pack and several excruciating therapy sessions she'd endured since. She slid the strap of her camp chair over her shoulder and walked slowly, careful to shift her weight to her cane until the muscles that had been torn and sewn back together loosened.

She found the perfect spot between the fences of two fields and settled down to watch both games.

"Oh, my God. Look what the dog dragged up."

Ryder stood and turned, smiling. The past years had been kind to her old friend, whose thick mane of dark hair and smooth olive skin were a testament to her Honduran heritage. "Desiree, as gorgeous and sexy as ever."

Petite but strong, Desiree wrapped her in a tight hug, then kissed her firmly on the lips. She stepped back. "Still a smooth talker. Let me look at you." She ran her hands down Ryder's arms and squeezed the hard biceps. "Damn, woman, you are better than fine." Desiree's gaze dropped to the brace around her knee. "What've you done to yourself, sexy?"

Ryder winked at her. "It's healing nicely, but you might want to watch the kisses. I can't run fast enough right now to get away from that big butch you married."

Desiree gave her a reproachful look. "We saw you on ESPN. I don't know what's wrong with you. Skyler taught you to ride big, beautiful horses, not bulls. Riding bulls is stupid. That's why men do it."

"The money's good and women crawl over each other to get in my bed."

Desiree clucked her tongue. "Your bed has never been empty. I should warn you. More than a few of your old conquests are around tonight."

"Well, I figure the statute of limitations has run out on anything I did twelve years ago."

"A woman's anger has no limitations." She folded Ryder's chair and tucked it under one arm while she hooked her other arm around Ryder's. "You better come with me so I can protect you. Lou and everybody are playing on field three."

She laughed at Desiree, who was half her size but twice as feisty. She missed this. It felt strange but really good to see her friends again.

Bridgette shook her head at Lou's call for a fastball. It was the top of the ninth inning with the score tied at five runs each. There were two outs and the count was two balls, one strike. Next up was the other team's slugger, and she was certain this batter would bunt to get on base and give the clean-up hitter a chance to break the tie.

Lou gave her the "whatever" signal and readied her crouch to catch the pitch, but Bridgette stared down the batter a second more, pleased to see her anxiously shift her weight toward the plate. Oh, yeah. She was going for a bunt.

Her windup was smooth, and when the screwball left her hand, she knew it would break perfectly to the inside. It glanced off the small end of the bat near the woman's hand to pop up and behind the plate. Lou scrambled after it without success and returned to the plate to signal for a curve ball. Bridgette shook her head. Lou's shoulders slumped and she stood and mumbled something to the umpire.

"Time," the umpire hollered.

Lou was the calm, steady partner that anchored a very volatile Desiree. But her face was a picture of sweaty frustration as she trudged out to the mound.

"I don't know what has crawled up your ass tonight, but you've disagreed with every pitch I've asked for," she said softly so the other team didn't hear. "On top of that, old man Denny has kneed me in the back before every pitch. We've gone two extra innings and my knees hurt, Bridge. Let's close this out."

She turned the ball in her glove and stared at the ground. Lou was right. She'd ignored some of the calls just because she wasn't in the mood to play softball tonight. Angry with herself over her breakdown in the studio, she was feeling cantankerous and contrary. She knew she was wrong, but she wasn't ready to lower her defenses. She gave Lou a hard stare.

"I knew she was going to bunt. She would have nailed a fast ball down the third-base line and outrun it."

Lou wiped her face on her sleeve, her expression the same as when she had to handle one of Desiree's moods. "I'm not implying that you've made bad decisions. You're the only one on this team who played college ball on a scholarship. Just tell me what you're going to throw so I'll be ready for it."

"She won't try to bunt because it'll be an automatic out if she fouls. If she crowds the plate, I'll give you that fastball you've been wanting all night. But I'm guessing she'll back up and swing away. So I'm planning to throw an off-speed drop ball."

Lou nodded. "Good plan."

She started toward the plate, but Bridgette called her back.

"You're second to bat when we get up next. If I strike this girl out, you have to promise to nail it to the fence so we can go home."

Lou grinned. "Honey, I'll hit it over the fence just so I don't have to run the bases on these tired old knees."

"Deal."

Obviously irritated that their consultation had stalled the game, the batter took her time knocking clay from her cleats for the tenth time, practicing her swing, and rearranging the dust in the batter's box. Bridgette waited calmly for her to settle in the back corner of the box, bat held high.

She slapped her glove loudly against her leg as she released the ball to sucker the batter into believing she'd thrown it hard. It almost worked. The bat dipped slightly, but the batter hesitated as she recognized the slower speed and drew back to adjust. What she failed to read was the drop as it broke the plate, and she swung at empty air.

The crowd, which had swelled as the other fields emptied, both cheered and groaned loudly. Bridgette accepted the high-fives of her teammates, then sank gratefully onto the bench in the back corner of the dugout. Lou plopped down, too, to pull off her shin guards and chest protector.

"Good job, ace."

"Thanks. Your turn now. Over the fence, you said."

Lou winked at her. "A promise is a promise."

"Hey, Lou. Who's Desiree's new escort?" Kristin, the youngest and newest member of the team, pointed toward the bleachers where a knot of players milled around Desiree and Ryder. Lou stood up, blocking Bridgette's line of vision.

"Well, I'll be mule-kicked. Wonder when that stray dog strolled into town."

"You know her?" Kristin twisted her fingers in her blond ponytail. "She's hot."

"Sure, that's—"

"Batter up!" The first batter had popped out on an infield fly, and the umpire was calling for Lou.

"On my way," Lou said, grabbing her bat and helmet.

Bridgette stood and elbowed through her tired teammates to the chain-link fencing that protected the dugout. "Come on, you guys. Pay attention." She cupped her hands around her mouth and yelled. "Outta the park, Lou. Better duck, pitcher."

The other players joined in the heckling as Lou rested the bat on her shoulder and watched a pitch go high and outside.

"Ball! Count is one and oh," the umpire said.

The pitcher nervously rubbed the ball against the leg of her shorts while Lou backed away and took a few practice swings. She grinned and pointed her bat toward Desiree and Ryder, then stepped up to the plate.

Bridgette heard the loud crack of the ball hitting the aluminum bat and the enthusiastic cheering around her, but her eyes were fixed on Ryder. The heat started in her belly and burned its way up to her cheeks. The dark cloud that had been following her all day instantly lifted.

She didn't move as the others poured out of the dugout to congratulate Lou. She was watching Ryder scan the team. Was she looking for her? Their gazes met and Ryder smiled.

"I can't believe that bitch has the nerve to show up here." Fran, the red-haired first baseman, hadn't left the dugout either.

"You know her?"

The team was sauntering back after shaking hands with the losers.

Trish, the second baseman, chimed in. "That's Marc Ryder. She's famous."

"More like infamous. Bitch has slept with everybody in town."

The venom in Fran's voice surprised Bridgette.

"I heard she was paralyzed from the neck down and stuck in some Texas nursing home," Vic, the centerfielder, said.

"Obviously, that isn't true. But if she wasn't standing right there, I'd have believed it after seeing that clip on ESPN," Trish said.

"ESPN?" Bridgette searched her memory for anything Ryder had said that might give her a clue. *I'm a professional rider.*

"She does rodeo. Rides bulls with the guys. She was ranked in the top ten but got messed up pretty bad a couple of months ago. They showed the clip about a million times. That bull threw her up in the air like a toy and stomped on her."

Bridgette grabbed the fencing and the rough chain-links cut into her fingers. Everything was spinning. *Rides bulls.* She couldn't breathe. She held on tight and took deep breaths to loosen the band of anxiety squeezing her chest. *She rides bulls.* She had to go. She had to leave before Ryder found her. She grabbed her equipment bag and headed for her car.

"Hey, Bridgette, wait up. Bridgette!"

She pretended she didn't hear Ryder calling to her or see her breaking away from her friends to limp after her. She stared straight ahead and walked faster, right into a young boy who was running to join his mother. Bridgette grabbed his arm before he fell to the ground. "Oh, gosh, I'm sorry. I didn't see you. Are you hurt?"

The boy's mother walked up. "He's fine. You know kids, they just take off without looking." She frowned down at her son. "What if that'd been a car instead of a person? You need to be more careful."

The boy brushed off his mother's scolding. "Sorry. Can I get some peanuts before we go?"

"Only if you walk and don't mow down anybody else." She rolled her eyes and turned to Bridgette as the boy took off in a sprint. "I'm sorry, and he will be, too, when I get him home."

"Really, don't be too hard on him. I wasn't looking either." She bent to pick up the equipment bag she had dropped. When she straightened, the woman was gone and she was face-to-face with Ryder.

"Hey." Ryder's cheeks dimpled and her teeth flashed white in the semi-darkness.

"Hello." Bridgette shifted her feet, searching for something to say. Damn. Ryder looked good. Better than good. She was dressed in tight stonewashed, boot-cut jeans and a crisp, white shirt with the sleeves rolled midway up her forearms. "About that art class—"

Ryder's smile dimmed. "Uh-oh. Trouble."

But she wasn't referring to what Bridgette was about to say. Bridgette barely had time to step out of the way as Fran stormed up.

"I've been waiting a long time to do this."

Bridgette jerked in surprise when Fran delivered a slap that left the outline of her hand on Ryder's cheek.

Ryder didn't move. She hadn't even flinched when Fran drew back to hit her.

"Now you have," she said. "And I owe you an apology. I'm sorry. But it was twelve years ago and we were just kids. Let it go."

Fran's eyes filled with tears. "I wish that bull had broken your worthless neck."

Bridgette was speechless as Fran stomped away.

"Sorry about that. Old history. We'd been out a few times when I got a job offer riding on the dressage circuit. I was eighteen and anxious to see the world and kind of left without telling her."

"It's none of my business."

"I just didn't want you to think…well, it doesn't matter. Have you eaten? Could I take you out for dinner or coffee and dessert?"

"Thank you, but no. I've got an early class tomorrow."

"Lunch tomorrow?"

"I'm busy." Bridgette started toward her car.

Ryder looked confused and hobbled after her. "You got my note, right? I had an appointment I couldn't miss. I would have called, but you didn't give me your phone number. I called the art school, but they wouldn't tell me either. I don't know when or where to show up for your class."

Bridgette stopped. "About that. We've hired a different model. You're off the hook." She started walking.

"Wait." Ryder grabbed her arm. "I thought we had fun."

She stopped again and faced Ryder. She would have never guessed this woman was stupid enough to play with bulls for a living. "It was fun. *Was* is the key word here."

"So we're a one-nighter?" Surprise, a flash of hurt, then challenge flashed across Ryder's handsome face. "Fine. I can do that. I just hadn't pegged you as that type."

"Then we're even. I'd never have guessed you were such an idiot either."

CHAPTER NINE

R yder blinked away the sweat that dripped into her eyes, then put her head down and pedaled hard and fast on the stationary bicycle. The muscles in her injured leg screamed, but she tightened the bike's tension another notch and rose to put her full weight onto her legs for one last climb.

Her quads bulged and her calves cramped from her hour-long workout, but she welcomed the punishing pain and exertion. The more she hurt, the less she thought about the sting of Bridgette's kiss-off.

I'd never have guessed you were such an idiot either.

What the hell did that mean? Had someone at the softball field said something that pissed Bridgette off?

It wasn't like she couldn't find plenty of other women to sleep with. Still, she replayed the night again and again in her mind, searching for something that she'd said or done wrong.

Forget it. There were no answers when somebody dumped you. Like her world-traveling parents, who abandoned her to be raised by her grandmother. Like her grandmother, who dumped her in a program for juveniles so she could paint without the needs of a child disturbing her.

She had learned early to hit the door first so you weren't the one left with a damaged ego. She was irritated that she hadn't seen it coming with Bridgette.

"Working that leg too hard, too soon is only going to set you back."

She was so absorbed in her thoughts, she hadn't seen Jessica come into the equestrian center's gym. She sat back onto the bike's saddle and slowed her feet to a cool-down pace.

"No pain, no gain," she said, accepting the towel Jessica offered to wipe the sweat from her face.

"A very wise physical therapist once told me that too much pain is a good indicator you're pushing too hard, too soon." Jessica's stare was curious. "You definitely looked like you were hurting."

She swiped at her face again, as if she could wipe away the expression that had betrayed her. "Nah. I just make weird faces when I'm concentrating." She could see that Jessica wasn't buying it, so she offered up her patented Ryder-style cocky grin she used to slam the door on her insecure little Marci Ridenhouer deep inside. "Did you come up for a swim?"

The gym complex included an indoor swimming pool and hot tub adjacent to the exercise room, and she could see a swimsuit under the terry-cloth robe Jessica wore loosely tied around her rather large belly.

"Seems like my back aches constantly these days, and the pool helps." She grimaced. "But I got a little dizzy in the water a couple of weeks ago, so Skyler made me promise I wouldn't swim alone until after the baby comes. I was hoping I could convince you to accompany me, so I don't have to ask her. She's got so much to do, trying to manage her work and most of mine, too."

Ryder climbed down from the bike. "Sure, I don't mind." Being around someone eight months pregnant did make her a little nervous, but she also felt curiously protective. "The pool will probably be good for me."

She'd never thought pregnant women were attractive, but Jessica was truly beautiful. Her thick black hair draped in a glossy cape across her shoulders and provided the perfect frame for her ice-blue eyes and radiant face. She was happy that Skyler had found this incredible woman, but she couldn't help being a little jealous of their bond. It was something she'd never had, would never have.

"Jacuzzi first, to loosen up my back," Jessica said.

Ryder frowned. She didn't know anything about being pregnant, but she'd read the warnings always listed at hotel pools. "I thought pregnant women weren't supposed to get in hot tubs."

"Skyler lowered the temperature so I'm safe for about ten minutes at a time."

Her skimpy spandex shorts and tank top were an adequate bathing suit, so Ryder carefully slid into the sunken Jacuzzi and reached up to help Jessica. When the terry robe dropped to the floor, she stared. A long white scar ran down Jessica's thigh, and several others crisscrossed her knee. When she looked up, Jessica was watching her.

"I know a little about leg injuries myself," she said, accepting Ryder's help stepping down into the water. "I have an artificial joint in my knee that ended my riding career."

"I'm sorry. I didn't know."

She was suddenly embarrassed that she hadn't kept in closer touch with her friends. She'd spent the past twelve years gallivanting around the world without a thought of the people she'd left behind. Had she grown up to be just like her parents?

"There was a time when I thought competing in the Olympics was the only thing that mattered in life." Jessica looked down at her belly to rub it. "Now, it seems so unimportant."

It hadn't occurred to her that more than money and family ties qualified Jessica to run the top-level equestrian center. "What happened? I mean, if you don't mind telling me."

"I don't mind." Jessica sank up to her chin in the heated water and sighed. "God, this feels good." She moved around until she found the seat with water jets that massaged her lower back. "It started with an accident on a cross-country jump. My horse broke his leg, and I broke mine. He was put down right there on the course, and I had two surgeries to pin my femur back together and later graft a new ACL in my knee."

"That's rough." She closed her eyes against unwelcome visions of Aintree's steeplechase course. She'd seen several incidents like that. The worst was a horse that broke his back. When she opened her eyes, Jessica was watching her. "I've seen a few of those accidents. They're not pretty."

They shared a moment of silence, both lost in their own ugly memories.

Ryder frowned. "I didn't realize an ACL could end a riding career."

"Actually, my ACL graft would have been fine if I'd taken time to properly rehab. But the trials for the US Equestrian Team were only months away."

Ryder shook her head. She could see where this was going. "I got stomped on the side of my leg. It broke my shin and dislocated my knee, but it only tore the ligament on the inside. The ACL was just stretched a bit. The worst part is the plate in my shin."

Jessica nodded and glanced up at the clock on the wall. "Help me switch to the pool?"

They began walking the width of the shallow end against the gentle resistance of the water. Ryder was careful to stay within reach in case Jessica slipped or faltered.

"So, how did you meet Sky?"

Jessica's smile was brilliant at the mention of Skyler. "You know, it's weird that we didn't meet years ago. Kate Parker and my mother were lovers when I was young, and, even when they split up, I still spent summers here with Kate. I stopped coming when I was about twelve and seriously training in Atlanta, where Mom and I lived. That's about the time Kate took Skyler under her wing."

"But I thought Kate and your mom were still together. Skyler said something about them being in Greece right now."

"Mom's paranoia split them up. When I got old enough to start school, she was afraid having two moms would make me a target for bullies. She also thought it might influence me to be gay. She was wrong on both counts. Since having me in the picture split them up, I was happy to be the catalyst to get them back together. Sky and I were training six days a week, so Mom had to come here to visit with me." Jessica chuckled. "I only needed to get them in the same room. After all those years apart, they were still in love."

Ryder tried to imagine the kind of love that could last for years. Only two people hadn't walked away from her. "Sky and Tory taught me how to ride."

"Sky's great with the kids. She'll be a wonderful parent." Jessica absently ran her hand over the child she and Skyler would raise together.

"Boy or girl?" Ryder asked.

"It's a girl, but we'd be happy with either."

"Oh, yeah. You guys mentioned that when I first got here. Is it rude to ask how you, uh, you know, did it?" Much to her consternation, she felt her cheeks heat. "I mean, did you go to a sperm bank?"

"I wanted our child to have something of Sky in her, so we convinced Douglas to make a contribution."

"Sky's twin?"

"Yes."

She laughed. "But he's a—"

"A very sweet, very accomplished math genius." Jessica's pointed glare made her feel like a reprimanded kid. She was going to be a great mom, too. "He's a professor at Princeton, you know."

"Really? Good for Douglas."

They completed their route and began again.

"But back to my story. My leg was barely healed when I showed up here with a new horse and Kate paired me with Skyler as a trainer."

"It was love at first sight, right?"

Jessica laughed. "Hardly. We butted heads a lot at first. Sky knew I wasn't ready, physically or emotionally, that soon after the accident. But I was determined. So determined that when the ACL graft began to fail, I started injecting it with numbing agent to keep jumping."

"I can't believe Skyler would let you do that."

"She didn't know. Anyway, I kept pushing until I completely ripped the graft and ruined the knee joint. I'm glad they could repair it enough with an artificial joint so I can still walk. I'm even more grateful that Skyler didn't hate me when she found out I'd been keeping it from her."

"So, the moral of your story is—"

"There are things—your quality of life, people who care about you—much more important than another trophy."

"Not for me. Riding is everything in my life. No girlfriend to tie me down. No family in the States since my grandmother died. According to the annual Christmas card, my parents are living somewhere in South Africa now. Hell, I don't even have a dog."

"You have Skyler and Tory. You're the sister their parents didn't give them." Jessica slipped a little on the slick pool bottom and Ryder caught her hand to steady her. When they continued, Jessica didn't let go. "And that makes you family to me and Leah, too."

She shrugged, unsure how to respond. She didn't know if she wanted friends who were like family. The family thing hadn't exactly worked out for her in the past. She held Jessica's arm tight as they exited the pool, then helped her slip back into her robe.

"Thanks. It may not seem like much, but that little bit of exercise really makes my back feel better. Seems like this little girl spends half her day kicking me in the kidneys," she said.

Jessica gave her a long look, her eyes kind. "We love having you here. Relax and give yourself time to fully heal."

She nodded, even though she knew she'd never have enough time for that to happen. A lot more than her leg needed healing.

Ryder stared up at the two-story brick mansion, unsure why she was standing here.

Maybe it was Jessica's talk about family and other things in life. Maybe it was her preoccupation with another artist that she couldn't seem to shake. Regardless of what had brought her to the doorstep of her grandmother's—now Ryder's—mansion, it was time to buck up and deal with it.

Eleanor White had been dead for nearly five years. Ryder was the only child of Eleanor's only child. But Eleanor never got along with her daughter, and Ryder's parents hadn't lived in the United States since they dropped her off like a stray kitten for Eleanor to rear. She guessed that was why Eleanor had designated her as the sole heiress to the multi-million-dollar estate.

But in the years since her grandmother's death, she'd hardly spent any of the money or set foot in the house and stables. She'd instructed her lawyer to continue contributing to the charities Eleanor had and to make sure the house and grounds were secure and tended as if someone still lived there.

Flowers bloomed in neat beds that surrounded the house and immaculate lawn. The long brick drive was well maintained and clear of any debris. Inside, the furniture was draped in white sheets, ghostly figures in the dim light. The hum of the central air-conditioning and the recent vacuum tracks on the carpets explained why the house smelled fresh despite being closed up.

She wandered from room to room, pulling out memories she had packed away and forgotten: Eleanor entertaining art patrons in the huge dining room and formal living room, Eleanor mixing colors in her cavernous studio, and her childhood bedroom suite that was both refuge and prison.

It seemed smaller than it had when she was eight years old. Still, how many children had a three-room suite? It wasn't like she brought friends home from school to play with her.

She couldn't really fault Eleanor. She had never intended to be a mother, much less a grandmother. She wasn't cruel, just severely bipolar.

Art was her lifeline. When she was depressed, she hid in her dark bedroom for weeks and painted tortured canvases by candlelight. When she was manic, she moved to her sun-filled studio and painted around the clock.

Ryder lived for the manic periods. At least Eleanor talked to her then and encouraged her to paint, too. She tried, but Eleanor was never satisfied with her own work, much less that of a child. Ryder's last attempt still sat on the easel in her playroom, surrounded by posters of the US Equestrian Team and shelves that held dozens of model horses.

Riding had been her lifeline. When she began to get into trouble at school, a concerned teacher convinced Eleanor that her granddaughter would get the attention she craved at the Cherokee Falls Equestrian Center. She wasn't one of the juveniles referred by social workers to Leigh Parker's program. Eleanor was wealthy enough to buy horses and pay for lessons. But Ryder was just as emotionally bruised as those other kids. She found friends there every day after school and on Saturdays, and Eleanor found the solitude she needed.

She wandered back into the studio, which reminded her of Bridgette's loft with tall, uncovered windows that flooded the room with natural light. Would Bridgette like this studio, too? She imagined her, blond curls falling across her shoulders, standing in the center, brush poised to transfer her emotions onto the canvas.

She closed her eyes. She could almost taste Bridgette, feel the softness of her breast against her cheek, and hear Bridgette's heart beating wildly.

Ryder shuddered. She'd rarely had a second thought about a woman after the tryst was over. Why now? Maybe it wasn't Bridgette she really wanted. Maybe it was all the other people who had walked out of her life, walked out of this mansion.

She would call the lawyer tomorrow and tell him to sell everything—the house, the furniture, and her grandmother's art.

Her life was simple now. She leased a furnished condo and kept few personal items other than her clothes and riding equipment. She could pack up in an hour and hop a plane to her next adventure when the mood hit.

No house to sell, no furniture to ship, no relationship to anchor her.

Chapter Ten

Bridgette hurried across the campus, barely noticing the October chill. Another red light and she would have been late to the evening class. It took longer than she had expected to find a new set of silk sheets. She bought deep blue to replace the red ones she had thrown out.

Hopefully, her teaching assistant had arrived early and was prepping the model Bridgette had suggested she enlist for tonight's class. His physique wouldn't offer the same lesson she'd planned to teach, but an androgynous model like Ryder was a rare find.

"Bridgette, a moment, please."

She gritted her teeth but stopped and forced a smile before she turned. "Dean Blanchard. What can I do for you?"

"I may have a good prospect for a donation to the auction."

"That's wonderful. I've put out some feelers myself and should have some results to report to the committee in a few days."

"Excellent. I knew you were the right person for the job."

"So who is your prospective donor?"

He gave her a smug look. "I've heard that Eleanor White's granddaughter is in town for the first time in years. She's the sole heir to that estate, and the old mansion is still filled with art."

"Eleanor White! She died almost five years ago. Her collection is intact?"

"Yes. The lawyer overseeing the estate is a friend, and he said the granddaughter apparently isn't interested in Eleanor's collection.

He's sure we could probably convince her to donate several pieces as a tax write-off."

"You haven't spoken with her yet?"

"No. He couldn't give me her cell number without her permission, but I have a number for the friends she's visiting. It's in my office. If you have a moment, I can get it for you. "

"You want *me* to call her?"

He frowned and pushed his hands into his pockets, obviously trying to decide how to phrase what he wanted to say. "My friend said, uh, she would be more readily agreeable if a woman made the proposal."

"A woman."

"Yes." He raised his chin and looked her in the eye, as if daring her to object to his honesty. "It seems that, like you, she prefers the company of women. And I understand that she's considered quite attractive to, uh, other women who prefer women."

"Dean Blanchard, you old dog. Are you proposing that—"

"I'm only suggesting that she would be more receptive to listening to a beautiful, passionate artist than a stuffy, old department head." He huffed. "For God's sake, I'm not asking you to date her. Just talk her out of some of her grandmother's paintings."

She chuckled at his consternation. "Okay, but I'm late to my evening class. I'll stop by tomorrow and get that number."

"Very well. Tomorrow will be soon enough."

Bridgette closed the door of the darkened classroom and waited for her eyes to adjust. She had only six students in this advanced sketch tutorial, and each sat before an easel positioned in focused pools of the track lighting. The only other lights in the room illuminated the small stage where the model's back was turned to the students.

She nodded to her assistant, Karen, who signaled that she was going to step out of the classroom for a few minutes. After she quietly laid her bag on the desk in the back of the room, she slipped a Bach CD into the small stereo on the shelf behind her. The music and the lowered lights relaxed and isolated the students from the hallway noise. These small touches, as well as her expertise, made Bridgette a favorite among the serious art students.

Her assistant had done well. The model was nude, except for a Greek-style helmet that covered the face turned toward the left. Feet shoulder-width apart, the model gripped a long spear planted parallel to the body, accentuating the well-developed bicep. The right hand rested on the model's hip, bulging the muscle at the top of the shoulder.

Bridgette frowned and narrowed her eyes. She had used this model before and insisted that he shave down for the job, but he'd never been this smooth before.

The timer went off and the stage went dark.

"Five-minute breather for the model. Students, you may continue sketching or take a break," she announced.

Karen returned to the classroom. "Great model, huh? I set up easels for us, too, if you want to sketch. I don't know where you found her, but that's an amazing body."

"Her? I thought I told you to call Jason because Ms. Ryder wouldn't be here."

"He couldn't do it. I was just about to call the agency to see if they could send someone but found a message in my mailbox that said Ms. Ryder had called to confirm she would be here after all. I thought the message was from you."

"No. She must have called the department secretary."

"Lucky for us, huh? It'll be fun to see who picks up on her gender before we switch to a frontal view next week."

"I don't think so." She didn't want to envision Ryder naked, facing her whole class. Sure, her students were artists and they'd drawn nude models before. But not a body she knew so personally. Not this body that she'd slept with. Fucked. Touched. Tasted. Drooled over.

"Don't think what?" Karen looked confused.

"Uh, I don't think she'll be back next week. I should have explained better. I had told her not to come tonight because she can't be here next week."

"Oh. I'm sorry. I misunderstood."

"Don't worry about it. I'll talk to her at the hour break."

The buzzer sounded again and the stage lights came on. The students worked frantically.

It was so clear now. How could she not have recognized that back, that ass the moment she walked in? Her breath caught.

They were faint and nearly healed, but those were definitely scratches across Ryder's left butt cheek. The vivid memory nearly stole her breath. Her nails digging into Ryder's ass, urging her to thrust harder, faster as she was about to come. Bridgette sat on the desktop and squeezed her legs together to stop the throbbing in her crotch. Heat rose up her neck and she glanced around to see if anyone noticed.

But they were all sketching. Karen, too. She took a few deep breaths and refocused on her job. She moved from student to student, offering suggestions, commenting on their work. When the buzzer sounded, she pulled the curtain to conceal the stage while Karen switched on the overhead lights.

"You've got twenty minutes to work on your sketches, and then the model will return with a different pose for the second half of class," she told her students before slipping behind the curtain to confront Ryder.

She picked up the robe tossed onto a padded bench that would be used for the next pose and held it up as Ryder pulled off the helmet. She put her finger to her lips and pointed to the door of her small office that served as a dressing room.

Ryder drew the robe around her shoulders but left it hanging open as she followed. Bridgette closed the door and whipped around to glare at her.

"What are you doing here?" she demanded in a hushed voice.

"I came to do what I said I'd do."

"Keep your voice down. These walls are thin."

Ryder's hair was soaked from wearing the metal helmet under the hot lights. Sweat trickled down her neck, between her breasts, and over the bands of her abdomen.

"Close your robe, please."

"I'm hot," Ryder said, exposing a breast as she lifted the terry-cloth collar to wipe her face. "Besides, it's nothing you haven't seen before." Ryder took a step closer and she breathed in her spicy scent. "Something I'd be happy to show you again, if you want."

God, she did want. Badly. This room was too small. Ryder was too close. She needed to get out of here.

"There's bottled water in the small fridge over there. I'd suggest that you drink enough to stay hydrated under the lights." She pointed to the right. "The bathroom's through that door." She was babbling. Ryder obviously was acquainted with the bathroom because that was where she'd stripped before the class started.

Bridgette pressed against the door at her back when Ryder took another step forward. The robe had fallen back on her shoulders, baring her breasts. Her taut nipples were so close, Bridgette could almost feel them touching her own. Ryder's eyes were liquid chocolate, her gaze melting.

"Don't," she whispered as Ryder's lips brushed hers.

"I can't help myself," Ryder murmured.

The kiss was slow and languid. Ryder's tongue was hot but her mouth gentle. She clutched Ryder's robe to push her away but instead pulled her closer. Pressed between the door at her back and Ryder's hard body, she whimpered and slipped her hand downward to clutch Ryder's firm ass. Carefully. No fingernails, no marks.

Ryder's fingers brushed her cheek and slipped around to grasp the back of her neck. The calluses of Ryder's hand were rough against her skin.

Then she remembered why Ryder had calluses on her right hand. She pushed her away.

"Stop. This is not going to happen."

"After class, then." Ryder's voice was hoarse.

"Never. It's not going to happen again. Ever." She smoothed her shirt and wiped at her lips, as though she could erase the kiss. "You have fifteen minutes before Karen comes back in and gets you ready for the next session. You'll pose for fifteen minutes, take a five-minute break, then pose for fifteen more. After that you're done."

"When's the next class? Karen said it was a two-night deal."

"You won't be here for a second night." She slipped out the door before Ryder could say more.

When the lights dimmed and the curtain was drawn back for the next session, she was pleased that Karen had carefully followed her instructions.

Ryder was a Greek warrior, lounging on the padded bench, propped up by her left arm, shoulders turned toward the students. Her healing left leg lay flat on the bench, while the right was bent to support her arm casually resting on her knee.

But she wasn't fully nude. Leather armor covered her shoulders and breasts. They had purposefully left off the matching belly plate to expose her muscled abdomen. Attached to the armor, a crimson cape draped down her back and swirled across her hip to discreetly cover her crotch.

Still, the female identity was obvious to Bridgette. The lack of body hair, the shape of the rib cage, elegant wrists, and finely boned hands were telling. Would her students recognize them?

Despite her frustration that Ryder was here, in her classroom, she reveled in the lesson this session would provide her budding artists.

The eye ports in the helmet were fathomless black holes under the stage lighting, but she could feel Ryder watching her. She stared back, careful to keep her expression stoic even though her mouth was parched and her heart pounded.

She watched the tight abdominal muscles contract and expand with each breath. Then they stilled, as though Ryder was holding her breath, and she realized she was unconsciously licking her dry lips. She ran her tongue over her lips again, inexplicably pleased when the muscles jerked, confirming she wasn't the only one affected by their proximity.

Feeling more in control, she went to the easel Karen had prepared for her and began to draw. Soon, she was immersed so deep, she sketched through the breaks and never looked up when Karen pulled the curtain on the stage and instructed Ryder how to exit without walking through the classroom after she dressed.

"Do you want to stay a while longer?"

She was surprised to glance up and see the classroom empty. Karen had already put the supplies away and stood near the door.

"I was about to head out," Karen said. "Do you need anything else?"

"No. Gosh. I didn't realize it was so late. You go ahead. I need to wash up. I'll lock the classroom."

She carefully stored the drawing in her office and washed the charcoal from her fingers. The robe and costume Ryder had worn lay across the short sofa. She stared at the crimson cloak and realized the color had not triggered another anxiety attack. In fact, she was so focused on Ryder, she hadn't even hesitated as she sketched the cloak. Relief flooded her, and she made a mental note to return the helmet and armor to the drama department tomorrow.

It was late when she stepped out into the cool evening, but she felt surprisingly good. A few students were still moving between the buildings and her car wasn't that far away. She hummed to herself as she walked, enjoying the clear night. Then she stopped.

A dark figure sat on the trunk of her car. She slowed and glanced about. A young couple sat a short distance away on a bench, so she wasn't alone. As she cautiously approached, the figure turned and the streetlight revealed Ryder's face.

She let out her breath and walked directly to the car.

"If you need a ride, I can call a cab for you," she said, unlocking the door. The hurt that flashed across Ryder's features made her instantly regret her caustic offer.

"I don't need a ride." Ryder slid off the trunk and hobbled around to face her.

She was surprised to see Ryder using the cane again. She hadn't had it in the art building. Standing while she posed for thirty minutes apparently had taken a toll.

"You're a real faucet, you know. Off, on. Hot, cold."

She sighed. "Marc, I don't want to hurt you."

Ryder's smile was bitter. "Good thing I've got a thick skin. But I always finish what I start. I told Karen I would be here next week to pose again."

"I won't need you next week. I've already promised someone else the job."

It was a small lie.

"I don't believe you."

She rubbed her temple. "Look. I don't usually know the models personally, and I realized tonight that I don't want you up there naked in front of my students. It makes me uncomfortable." Her earlier euphoria evaporated. She suddenly felt tired and deflated. "You make me uncomfortable."

"I like the way you say Marc," Ryder said softly.

Damn it. She wasn't listening.

"I don't want to go out with you. I don't want to sleep with you again. Please leave me alone."

This was a big lie.

She crossed her arms over her chest and stared at her feet, refusing to meet Ryder's gaze. There was a long silence.

"I won't bother you again."

She stayed propped against her car until she heard the diesel engine of the truck parked nearby rumble and didn't look up until she was sure Ryder was gone.

CHAPTER ELEVEN

W̶ell, well, well. You must be the big bad bull rider the children are all talking about."

Ryder turned from brushing Wind Walker to study the attractive redhead who was assessing her, undressing her with every sweep of her gaze. "I'm Ryder." She brushed her lips against the back of the woman's hand. "At your service."

"That's what I've heard."

"Not from the children, I hope."

"No. They wouldn't know of such things. But your reputation has preceded you."

"Has it?" She stepped closer. The woman's perfume was expensive. Her riding breeches hugged her curves like a BMW on a mountain road. "And you are?"

"Alexandra."

Ryder's interest—and other parts—swelled. *A redhead with big tits, the impulse control of a two-year-old, and the sex drive of a teenage boy.* She cocked her head, letting her gaze settle on Alexandra's full breasts. "Exactly what does the rumor mill say about me?"

Alexandra traced her fingers along the muscled shoulder exposed by her black racer-back tank. "That you are strong and a fantastic rider." Her hand trailed down and tugged at the waistband of Ryder's jeans. "Rumors say you can give a lady a good ride, too." Alexandra's smile was predatory. "But maybe I should find out for myself."

She moved closer, forcing Alexandra to step back. "A lot of rumors aren't true." Another step and Alexandra was against the side of the stall. "But I can guarantee that one is."

Alexandra lifted her chin, her eyes challenging. "I'll be the judge of that."

Ryder thrust her hips forward, pinning Alexandra against the oak paneling. She drew the shimmering red hair back and lowered her head so that her words, her breath washed over the pulse throbbing in Alexandra's neck. "I think I should be the one to judge. I've heard a few things about you, too." Alexandra's neck arched toward her, as though seeking her kiss. But she denied her, keeping the sliver of distance between skin and lips.

The tables had turned between predator and prey, and Alexandra whimpered. "What have you heard?"

She slid a thigh between Alexandra's legs and pressed against the heat of her crotch. "That you are one bad girl." She rolled her hips and nipped hard at the plump earlobe. Word around the barns was that this one liked it a bit rough. "Bad girls sometimes need to be punished." Another whimper, accompanied this time by a deep shudder. "Are you a bad girl, Alex?"

"Yes," she hissed. "I'm very bad. I cheat on my husband because he doesn't give me what I need."

"Tell *me* what you need."

Alexandra seemed hesitant, her voice breathy. "I need to be spanked. I need to be pulled across your lap and spanked. Then fucked, hard, really hard."

She bit down on the soft flesh of Alexandra's neck and encouraged the jerking hips with her hands. "I can give you what you need. I can redden your ass and fuck you until you can't sit down." She abruptly stepped back, leaving Alexandra to thrust against empty air. "But not here. I need privacy and a bit of equipment."

Alexandra's face was flushed, her expression briefly stunned. She stared at Ryder. "I know a place. It has everything we need."

"This is good, Bridgette. I like it."

Leah surveyed the series of sketches Bridgette had taped to the wall.

"When I was watching Sure get the best of the larger colt, I thought maybe this could be a lesson on dealing with bullies or a story about learning to accept who you are, use the talents you have, it takes all sizes and types to make a team. Something along those lines."

Leah nodded and pursed her lips. "The bully theme is important but a little overdone. I like the team idea. It's more positive."

"I like the teamwork idea, too. I could throw in a soccer ball." She flipped the pages of her sketchpad to a clean sheet.

"A soccer ball. I like that." Leah opened her laptop on the desk and surveyed Bridgette's drawings again while it booted up. "We could start with the yearlings observing a group of kids playing soccer. Sure is standing at the fence, watching, when his friends join him and they get the idea to snitch a ball and see if they can kick it around."

"Gotcha." Bridgette began to sketch as Leah sat at the desk and typed out the story in her head.

They both looked up at the sound of a door slamming and footsteps. Leah glanced at the ceiling.

"Must be Skyler. There's an apartment overhead that was hers before she moved into the house with Jessica. She's probably looking for something she left up there."

Although Leah and Bridgette both had work spaces in their homes, they found the office in Creek Barn, with the smell of leather and hay all around them, stimulating when creating their popular children's stories about Leah's Chincoteague yearling.

When they offered to donate ten percent of their book royalties to the Young Equestrian Program in exchange for work space, Skyler was happy to share her old office since she mostly worked out of the main office in the house now.

They heard more bumping above, then giggling.

Leah paused her typing. "You don't think it's some of the older kids, do you? No telling what they're doing up there."

A low moan, then murmuring. Bed springs squeaked and several thumps sounded, like shoes hitting the floor. It was pretty clear that whoever was up there wasn't rummaging through a closet for lost boots.

Leah reached for the cordless phone and ran her finger down the list of speed dials taped next to it on the desk. "I'll call—"

"That's right, baby. I'm a bad girl. You need to punish me."

Leah growled and slammed the phone down. "That's not kids up there."

Bridgette laughed. "You recognize the 'bad girl'?"

A loud slap and squeal, then a low murmur. "I have. I've been a very bad girl."

Bridgette choked back a laugh and shook her head at the breathy declaration.

"I should have guessed," Leah said, shaking her head, too. "That's Alexandra. I swear that slut will jump anything that's breathing."

"I'm surprised Skyler lets someone like that around with all the kids here in the afternoons."

"The only good thing I can say about her is that she has a strict nineteen-or-older rule, and her husband's a significant donor to the Parker Foundation. As long as the bitch keeps her hands off the kids, Skyler, and Tory, whatever else she does isn't my business."

A rapid series of slaps and squeals had them both covering their mouths to stifle their laughter.

"Damn, I wish I had a recorder on me," Leah said. "Sounds like she's getting exactly what she deserves."

The slapping slowed as the squeals became whimpers, then finally stopped, and Bridgette turned back to her sketch. What she saw when she looked at the blank paper, however, wasn't horses. She shifted in her chair. She was having difficulty seeing anything other than a woman stretched over the lap of a lover, her pale buttocks marked with red handprints.

She snuck a sideways glance at Leah, glad to see she wasn't the only one flushed and shifting in her seat. She took a deep breath and scanned the drawings she had taped on the wall in an effort to fill her thoughts with horses instead of what was going on overhead. Leah began typing on her laptop, and the familiar sound helped Bridgette refocus.

Then the squeaking started. Random at first, then a steady rhythm. Throaty moans. Definitely Alexandra. Deep murmurs. Not Alexandra.

Leah clicked her mouse a few times and soft music drifted from her laptop to cover the noise. She resumed typing, and Bridgette began to draw.

"Harder, fuck me harder. Yes. Pound my pussy with that big thing. That's it." A second of quiet, low murmurs, then slapping, but less sharp. *Smack, smack, smack* joined the *bump, bump, bump* of the bed against the wall.

The moaning grew louder, joined by growls and grunts. The sexual symphony drowned out Leah's soft music.

"Oh, for Christ's sake." Leah grabbed a broom that was propped in the corner and used the handle end to thump loudly against the ceiling. "Hold it down up there," she yelled.

"Oh, God, oh, God. I'm coming, I'm coming. Don't stop." Alexandra's scream was shrill.

Bridgette gathered her things. "I'm sorry, Leah, but I can't work with that racket. My concentration is totally blown."

"Yeah. Mine, too." Leah began shutting down her laptop.

"Why don't we meet at my loft tomorrow afternoon and start work on a storyboard?"

"Sounds good. I'll try to have an outline and maybe some rough dialogue ready."

Leah was locking the office door when footsteps and voices sounded from the stairway.

"Sorry to hurry off, but I've got to go shopping this afternoon before I make nice with some of my husband's business clients tonight. I hate these dinners, but he pays the bills so I have to play the dutiful wife."

"Not a problem. I promised to meet Jess at the pool again to help her with her exercises."

Bridgette froze at the sound of the second voice. Ryder? What was she doing here? *An injury. She's a professional rider…I told Sky to call her up and insist she come here to rehab.* Crap. She flashed back to the woman riding the white stallion. Of course. That's why Ryder had seemed familiar when she saw her in the art gallery. She was wearing the same tight black T-shirt, just as she was now.

"God. I'm glad Edward never wanted children. I don't think I could stand to be pregnant. It's so disgusting," Alexandra said.

"Jess is beautiful—" Ryder stopped as they emerged from the stairway.

"Bridgette." Her face flushed a deep red as she stared at them. "Someone was banging—"

"That would be me." Leah's voice dripped sarcasm. "We were trying to work in the office, but your bad girl's little punishment session made it impossible to concentrate."

"She's not my...I didn't know anyone else was here," Ryder said weakly, her eyes begging Bridgette to understand. "Fuck. It was just a one-time thing."

Alexandra looked from Ryder to Bridgette. "Oops. Have I been poaching again?" Her sugar-sweet smile was insincere. "Sorry."

She stood on the toes to kiss Ryder's cheek and run her fingers through Ryder's hair. "I'm going to have a hard time forgetting you, stud, especially every time I sit down tonight."

She hurled Bridgette an arrogant look. "You lesbians really should keep a tighter rein on your butches." She laughed. "But then, that would spoil my fun, wouldn't it? Toodles, ladies."

"Bitch." Leah's growl bounced off Alexandra's back as she left.

Ryder took a step toward Bridgette. "I didn't—"

Leah moved between them in a protective stance and glared at Ryder. "Obviously you did. We, unfortunately, had front-row seats."

"I have to go," Bridgette said, turning away. She was tossing her art bag into the passenger seat of her car when Leah caught up to her.

"It's just a guess, but I get the impression you two know each other."

"Yes."

Leah was a friend, but she didn't feel like sharing right now. She was burning with jealousy, but she had no right, no claim. She had sent Ryder away. She had walked away from other women before. She hadn't blinked an eye when Tory chose Leah over her. So why did she feel so wounded this time? She and Tory had actually dated. She and Ryder had a one-night stand. There was nothing between them. At least that's what she'd told Ryder. That's what she'd told herself.

"Are you two dating?"

"No." Bridgette's laugh was a harsh bark, even to her own ears. "We had a fling. She posed as a model for one of my art classes."

Leah looked thoughtful. "Appears like it was more than a fling. You both seem upset."

"We had fun. That was it." She slammed the car door and walked around to the driver's side. She needed to leave, to be alone to stuff her emotions back into the dark prison where she'd guarded them the past few years.

But she also knew that Tory was a friend of Ryder's and it wasn't fair to let Leah think Ryder had broken any promises. "I was the one who told her one night was all there was between us. I'm just irritated that we couldn't get more done. I love working on the books with you, but I've got a lot of things to do for the auction, too."

"I might be able to help you with that. I have some media contacts that could generate some publicity for the event."

"That would be wonderful, Leah. We can talk about it tomorrow. Around two o'clock?"

"See you then."

Ryder stood in the shadows of the barn entrance and watched Bridgette drive away. She frowned when Leah spotted her and sauntered over.

"Well, Romeo, you managed to screw that up royally."

"What'd she say?" Even though Bridgette had refused to be with her again, she was always on the edge, sometimes at the center, of Ryder's thoughts. "She hates me, doesn't she?"

Leah studied her and Ryder shifted restlessly under her scrutiny.

"She's upset that we weren't able to get much done. She's got a lot of demands on her time right now, and your rather vocal tryst with Alexandra wasted the afternoon for her."

Ryder hung her head. "What'd she tell you about us?"

"She said you had a one-night stand. Was it more than that?"

She stared down the empty driveway. "No. I guess that was it."

CHAPTER TWELVE

Bridgette slammed the door and dropped her bag at her feet. She stood in the middle of the loft, filled with uncertainty. She'd never felt so discombobulated.

Mentally exhausted, she wanted to lie down on her bed and close her eyes to shut out the world. But the touch of silk sheets would only conjure visions of Ryder hovering over her, fierce yet tender, taking and at the same time filling her. No. She wouldn't go to the bedroom.

She felt rudderless.

She'd traveled the world most of her life, as a child with her parents and often alone as an adult. She had no answer when people would ask, "Where're you from?" Even then, she'd never felt adrift. Her safe place, her home base, was the tranquil center that she could find within herself whenever, wherever she simply sat down and meditated on being still.

Her balcony was her favorite place to meditate. A tall glass of wine and the sound of the stream trickling below might restore her calm. But her gaze fell on the wine rack and all she could see was the missing bottle she had shared with Ryder while she paged through the sketchpad. No. She could not be still. Not while her center was a tornado of twisting, churning emotions.

Then it came to her, a vision so pure and sharp that her fingers twitched with urgency.

Three hours later, the clay figure of a Grecian woman warrior had taken shape, and Bridgette began to carefully tool the details of a full-face helmet, a flowing cape, and a lean, toned physique. If she couldn't push the thoughts out of her head, then she would let them flow through her artist's hands.

Those hands were beginning to cramp now, after hours of frantic work. The sculpture wasn't completely finished, but she sat back and considered what she had created. Though the figure stood at ease, her subtle shaping of the muscles gave the distinct impression of coiled, barely restrained power. It was good. Very good. Probably the best work she'd done in years.

Her stormy emotions had calmed, and she put down her sculpting knife to stretch her arms overhead. She was hungry. Ravenous, actually. She had two hours before she had to meet with the auction committee on campus, so she decided to clean up and have a sandwich and latte at her favorite coffee shop downtown.

Bridgette put in her order and turned to search for an empty table in the busy coffee shop. All were filled, so she glanced at the back area where a short couch and several overstuffed chairs clustered around a coffee table. All seats were taken, but one of the two wingback chairs flanking a small table in the corner of the room was open. She glanced at the other chair, startled when Ryder met her gaze.

Bridgette had turned to request her order to go when a man at the front of the store stood to leave. Relieved that the table was on the other side of the room, she intentionally settled in a chair that put her back to Ryder. Still, she could feel Ryder's eyes on her, and her cheeks flushed hot as she flashed back to the spanking and moaning that had filtered down through the ceiling of the barn office.

She didn't want to think about that. She needed a distraction. While she waited for her food, she pulled out her notes to compile the agenda for the evening meeting.

"Turkey and cheese on wheat with cucumbers and sprouts and an iced Red Eye?"

"Yes, that's mine." Bridgette moved her papers aside and looked up as Ryder slid the dinner order on the table.

"I intercepted your waitress. I would have figured you for a chai latte kind of girl."

"There are a lot of things you don't know about me."

"I'm willing to learn if you give me a chance. I could use another friend."

"You don't seem to have any trouble finding new friends."

Ryder flushed. She looked down at the table and cleared her throat. "I'll understand if you tell me to get lost again. I just wanted apologize for earlier."

She sipped her coffee and stared at Ryder. "You don't owe me an apology. What you do isn't any of my business."

"I'm sorry I interrupted your work."

But not sorry that we overheard the details of you fucking that woman? Not sorry that just last night, you were begging me to sleep with you? She was angrier at her surprising and irrational jealousy than at Ryder's behavior. She had no claim, no right.

The ringing of her phone stopped her retort and she glanced at the caller ID. "I have to take this."

Instead of leaving, Ryder sat in the chair across from her.

"Hello?"

"William Blanchard here, Bridgette. I know you have a committee meeting tonight and I wanted to give you that name I mentioned last week. Eleanor White's granddaughter?"

"Yes. I'm sorry. I forgot to come by and get the phone number."

"I believe you may know the people she is staying with."

"Really? Well, that should make things easier. Hold on a second while I get a pen." She pushed her food aside and pulled her auction notes in front of her to write down the name. "Go ahead. Yes. I'm sorry. Can you spell it for me? At the equestrian center? I was just there this morning. I'll phone right after my meeting. Yes. Thank you."

She ended the call. Ryder was looking at her curiously.

"Is someone besides you visiting Jess and Skyler?"

"No. Who are you expecting?"

"William must have his information wrong. We're trying to get in touch with Eleanor White's granddaughter. Somebody told him she was staying at the equestrian center. Her name is Marci..." She looked down to check her note.

"Ridenhouer," Ryder said, her voice flat.

Her earlier anger evaporated and she wanted to laugh at the comically sour expression on Ryder's face. "You know her?"

"I *am* her. At least, I was. The first thing most kids do when they turn eighteen is register to vote. I went to the courthouse to have my name changed."

"Marci isn't that bad." She couldn't stop her smile.

"Do I look like a Marci to you?"

"No. I'd have to say Marc fits you much better."

"Thank you." Ryder's expression softened. "I've missed your smile," she said quietly.

Bridgette looked down at the table. "This is awkward."

"Smiling?"

"No. The favor I have to ask." When she looked up, she expected to see Ryder's usual smug grin. Instead, her expression was serious.

"Bridgette, I regret a lot about this afternoon. If I can do something to make it up to you, just ask it."

"It's not for me." It seemed important to say that. She didn't want this to be a personal favor. "It's for the art department. The college trustees plan to siphon money from existing departments to fund the new areas of study in an effort to enroll more students. The cuts they want to make in the art department are just unacceptable. We'll lose almost fifty percent of our art scholarships and ten percent of our faculty, including my artist-in-residence position."

Ryder shook her head. "Eleanor would have been furious. The reputation of the art program is what put that college on the map."

"Exactly. I've been appointed to organize an auction to raise money for an art endowment independent of the college's finances, money the trustees can't touch."

"You're going to auction off the art in the gallery?"

"No. Everything in the gallery technically belongs to the college, not the art department. We have to solicit artwork donated specifically for the endowment. Dean Blanchard was told you're heir to your grandmother's estate, and he's hoping I can talk you into donating a painting or two."

Ryder nodded and rocked in her seat thoughtfully. "That old house is filled with art. Not just Eleanor's."

"Can I tell the committee you'll make a donation?"

"I want two things."

"What?" She was confused.

"I want you to be my date to the auction."

"It'll be formal. No cowboy boots."

"I've been to gallery openings. You'd be surprised how well I clean up."

"Okay. I'll go to the auction with you, but you should know that I'll have duties to take care of—circulating among the guests, sucking up to big donors and such."

"Understood."

"What else?"

"I want to model for your class again tomorrow night as we originally agreed. Afterward, we can go to the mansion and you can pick out what you want for the auction."

She frowned. "Marc, I told you—"

"Do you want a donation?"

"Yes, of course."

"Then I'll see you in class tomorrow night." Ryder stood. "I'll let you finish your dinner so you can go to your meeting."

"Tomorrow, then." What else could she say?

CHAPTER THIRTEEN

The room was already darkened and the students were busily sketching in their individual pools of light. Ryder lay on her back, her far leg bent to turn her body slightly toward the students. One hand lay across her perfect belly, her fingers just touching the dark curls at her apex. The other formed a fist, gripping the sheet draping the padded bench. Her head was thrown back, hanging slightly off the end, her lips parted, her eyes closed.

Bridgette had intentionally arrived late to avoid talking with Ryder, but she couldn't boycott her own class. She moved silently among the students, taking notes. Halfway through the two-hour class, the buzzer sounded and she stepped onto the stage to draw the curtain. This time, she stayed in the classroom and turned up the lights while Karen slipped backstage to assist Ryder.

"How many of you figured out last week that this model is female?"

Two of the six students raised their hands. One was a male graduate student, the most experienced and most promising artist in the group. The other was a young woman Bridgette suspected was a lesbian.

"What tipped you off, Julie?"

The girl wrinkled her nose. "She wasn't hairy like a man. I guess that was the big thing."

"Male swimmers sometimes shave down for competition. Professional dancers wax their backs and chests to be smooth for their performances. So that's a guess, not conclusive evidence. What else?"

Julie shrugged and struggled to put her impressions into words. "I dunno. I could just tell. She's got a lot of muscle, but still different from man." She lifted her chin as if daring anyone to make a rude remark. "My girlfriend is a basketball player at Tech. Her muscles are hard, but there's still something about her that's softer, smoother than a man."

"Your instincts are good, but I'm looking for something a little more specific. Jason?"

"I think it was the smaller feet, the hands, the wrists, and the contour of the torso that gave it away for me."

"Explain that for the class."

"Even though the model has dark hair, there was no visual trace of hair on her fingers or toes. Men who shave down usually forget that part. Also, you can see the finer bone structure of the model's wrist and hands."

"It's not typical, but some women do have large hands and feet. What about the contour of the torso?"

"Although she has narrow hips for a woman, the spine curves more than a man's typically does and accentuates the tilt of the pelvis. Also, the helmet didn't hide her neck. The curve into the shoulder and the lack of a prominent Adam's apple is indicative of a woman. You can discount each of these things individually, but they add up to the subject being female."

"Very good." She clapped. "Let's take a ten-minute break and come back for one final pose."

As the students filed out, she resisted the impulse that tugged her toward the office where she knew Ryder would be resting and hydrating. She didn't want to be alone in that small room with Ryder naked under a thin robe. Instead, she walked around the room, writing and attaching Post-it notes of her observations on each student's sketch. When they all had returned, she lowered the lights and then sat on her desk at the rear of the room.

At her nod, Karen pulled the curtain back to reveal Ryder, sitting on the low bench, her feet crossed at the ankles, her body slouched to the left, propped up by one arm. Her right hand rested casually on her right leg, and Bridgette instantly imagined her own fingers resting on the smooth, warm thigh. Her breath hitched when Ryder's hot gaze found her in the darkness and blazed with desire as palpable as a touch to her skin. Without breaking their connection, she reached for her pad and charcoal. Then she mentally stepped back and began to draw.

She was so absorbed, she barely registered the sound of the buzzer and the overhead lights flicking on an hour later. She continued, filling in the details that were burned into her memory.

"Still up for a shopping trip through Eleanor's collection?"

She looked up from the naked Ryder in her drawing to the live version clothed in jeans and her usual black T-shirt. She couldn't stop her smile.

"Is your entire wardrobe jeans, white shirts, and black T-shirts?"

"I prefer to keep my life as simple as possible."

She carefully closed her sketchbook so the drawing wouldn't smear and slid it into her shoulder bag. There was nothing simple about what was going on between them.

Ryder unlocked the door and moved through the downstairs, flicking on lights.

"She has artwork in almost every room, so you may want to take notes about what you like and where it's located."

Bridgette pulled a notepad and pen from her bag, immediately looking at the large abstract hanging on the opposite wall. "Is that one of your grandmother's?"

"Yeah. It's from her Jackson Pollock stage. Eleanor may be best known for her impressionist paintings, but her personal favorites were always abstracts."

She stood before the canvas, evaluating the brushstrokes, the mixture of colors.

"She was an abstract kind of person. Complicated…like you." Ryder was standing behind her, too close. Goose bumps ran down her arms and raised the fine hairs on the back of her neck. She ignored the comment and jotted down a few things before moving to the next painting.

"Have you always called your grandmother by her first name?" She wasn't judging, just curious.

"She didn't like being a grandmother. She said it made her feel old."

"You mean she didn't like to be called Grandma because it made her feel old."

Ryder opened a door and led her into a sunroom filled with soft pastel paintings. "No. She didn't like *being* a grandmother. I think my parents dumped me here to get back at her for my mother's childhood."

She stopped writing and stared at Ryder. "So you grew up here? Where were your parents?"

Ryder shrugged. "Traveling around the world. Italy, Greece, Ireland, China. They live in South Africa now. At least that's where the card was postmarked last Christmas. My father makes his living in the import-export trade. When I was old enough to go to school, they decided it would be better if I lived in one place rather than following them around."

"My parents lived all over the world, too, but my brother and I were always with them."

Ryder waved her hand, dismissing the conversation. "Eleanor's studio is upstairs. We can take the back staircase from the kitchen."

Like Bridgette's studio, floor-to-ceiling windows covered one wall of the huge room. A large cabinet built into the wall was still packed with art supplies. Everywhere, blank and finished canvases were stacked in wire racks and against the walls.

"She was very prolific." Bridgette sorted through some finished canvases, pulling several out of the rack for a better look.

"Eleanor was bi-polar. When she was depressed, she would stay in her bedroom for weeks, painting maybe one canvas by candlelight. But when she was in a manic phase, she painted incessantly, hardly stopping to sleep or eat." Ryder sat on a tall stool positioned next to an easel with a half-finished canvas. "She would paint fast and furious, picture after picture. Consequently, some aren't very good, and others are incredible."

She stopped sorting and looked at Ryder. "Who took care of you? Did she have a housekeeper?"

"Nah. She had a cleaning service that came once a week. She would lock herself in here or in her bedroom while they were in the house."

She couldn't imagine what it must have felt like to be a small child in that big house with the only adult locked in a dark bedroom or painting away her days and nights. She'd had a wonderful childhood, living in fantastic places with her very nurturing parents and a loving brother.

"Who fed you? Put you to bed? Got you up and ready for school every day?"

"I didn't need anybody to take care of me. I took care of myself." The bitterness in her words surprised Bridgette. The crack in Ryder's confident, casual façade was like a blast of chill air. "I mean, she didn't let me go hungry. I was only six years old when my parents dumped me, and Eleanor knew she couldn't take care of me when she was depressed. The first thing she taught me was how to make a peanut-butter-and-jelly sandwich. When she was in her manic phase, she would overstock the pantry and fridge with things I could get for myself."

"Marc." She put her notepad down and went to her, but Ryder got up and walked to the windows to stare out at the night.

"Anyway, I was about thirteen when Eleanor signed me up for riding lessons at the equestrian center. It saved my life. It wasn't long before I was practically living there. Kate Parker never asked questions or turned me down when I wanted to stay overnight. Sometimes I'd stay a week or more, and Eleanor never seemed to notice I'd been gone."

Her heart ached for that lonely child, for this adult she hadn't realized was scarred by life, too. She wrapped her arms around Ryder and pressed her length against the stiff back. Ryder's hands were cold as they pressed over hers.

"That's where I met Tory and Skyler. They were a few years older, but I tagged along behind them like a bratty little sister." She took a deep breath and let it out. "They're like family to me, and I guess I'm still a bit of a brat."

She turned, her eyes imploring, the calluses on her fingers rough as she stroked Bridgette's cheek. "I am so, so sorry about that thing with Alex. I wouldn't normally care. But for some reason, I want you to think better of me."

"Marc." The voice that had screamed for her to run away was no match for the inexplicable force that compelled her to touch, to feel this woman.

Ryder shivered. "I want to kiss you." Her breath whispered across Bridgette's face.

"Yes."

Ryder's lips were reverent, brushing, touching so softly that she wanted to weep. She pressed her hips against Ryder's heat. She wanted more. She wanted Ryder to thaw the cold places she had guarded for so long. She wanted to heal Ryder's wounds.

"Please, Marc."

She was swept into Ryder's strong arms and they were moving out of the studio and down the hallway. The pulse throbbing in Ryder's neck tasted of salt and sweat. She shuddered as she flashed back to her classroom and the gorgeous body stretched naked under the hot stage lights.

She was on her feet again and Ryder's mouth found hers. Slowly their tongues danced. She pulled at Ryder's T-shirt, snaking her hands under it. The bands of Ryder's abdomen jumped under her fingertips.

"Bridgette, Bridgette. Wait." Ryder grabbed her hands and held them tight in hers. "I want…I need you to know something first. But I'm afraid you'll take it wrong."

"What is it? What do I need to know, darling?" They were standing next to a bed, and she blinked to adjust to the muted light coming from the hallway.

Ryder's eyes darkened at the endearment. "We can stop now and you can walk out the front door. But the paintings, any of them or all of them if you want, are yours."

"You think I would sleep with you because I want your paintings?" She felt like she'd been slapped and tried to pull away, but Ryder wouldn't release her.

"No. I don't," she said quickly, and then her tone softened. "That's what I need you to know. I *don't* think you would sleep with me in exchange for Eleanor's art." Ryder slowly released her hands and pulled her close. "This is about, I don't know, whatever this is that draws us to each other."

She rested her head against Ryder's shoulder. She felt it, too, but didn't dare speak of it. That would make it too real. Instead, her answer was a kiss, long and soft.

They undressed each other slowly, kissing and touching leisurely.

When Ryder lowered her to the bed, Bridgette pulled her down, too, covering herself with Ryder's flesh, entwining her lithe legs with Ryder's muscled ones. Ryder was hard against her soft body, hot against her cool skin.

Ryder caressed and tasted every inch of her until she thought she would burst with everything that welled up inside her.

"Marc. Marc." She moaned and dug her fingers into Ryder's hair as she slipped lower, feathering kisses across her belly and thighs.

She screamed as Ryder claimed her with her mouth and fingers. Then she reveled in the shudder of Ryder's body when she wrapped her legs around Ryder's hips and urged her to slide her hard clit against the slick evidence of her climax.

Ryder's eyes were bright as they bore into hers, showing her, feeding her the fire she stoked with each slow, careful thrust. When they came together this time, she glimpsed something different than hunger or victory in Ryder's gaze. Something like...surprise.

But when they collapsed together, Ryder tucked her face against Bridgette's neck, trembling in the aftermath of their coupling. She stroked the long, sweaty back and skated her hands over Ryder's perfect ass. God, she loved that ass.

"Say it again."

"What, darling?"

"My name. I love hearing my name on your lips."

Ryder's hips convulsed when she raked her nails over the smooth buttocks. "Marc. It's a beautiful name. It suits you."

Ryder's lips were on her throat, then her mouth. But Ryder's eyes were shuttered this time, dark thick lashes shielding the emotion Bridgette didn't want to see anyway.

Their kisses grew heated and purposeful again, and she rolled Ryder onto her back.

"My turn," she said.

When Ryder woke, the thin rays of dawn were filtering through the sheer drapes. She was alone with only Bridgette's sandalwood scent lingering on the blanket she had pulled from a closet and the pillow that had cradled her beautiful face.

Her hips jerked and she grew wet at the memory of Bridgette's fingers filling her, her mouth sucking her, her strokes taking her to that edge of passion again and again, only to deny her orgasm. She had begged shamelessly, even wept when her release was at last permitted. And then, Bridgette began again, claiming her four more times before Ryder was too depleted to respond.

Their first time had been about lust, passion burning hot and bright between them. This time had been about touching deeper places that spoke of caring and hinted at owning.

Now Bridgette was gone.

She sighed.

Nothing had changed. She was still the child nobody really wanted. She was the lover no one thought to keep. They all wanted her lust. None wanted her heart.

For a moment, Bridgette had touched, filled the empty places inside her. Now they ached with a new, sharper desolation. She had done what she swore she would never do again.

Damn it. She had let herself hope.

The door to her loft slammed behind her, but this time Bridgette felt no uncertainty. Her paints, her clay called to her. She was hungry and needed to shower, but her urgency would not let her stop to take care of those baser needs. She would paint with the scent of their passion still on her hands, on her cheeks, on her body.

It was her inspiration.

Art had always been an outlet for her.

After her brother died, the desolate feelings she poured onto canvas were tortured pictures that magnified rather than purged her agony. That work had made her reputation and filled her bank account. But it had also pushed her into a depression so deep, she had packed the last of those paintings away and spent more than a year in a monastery retreat where she learned to separate and shut away those dark thoughts to find peace from her pain. When she began to paint again, the raw passion that marked her earlier work was gone, locked away with the torment of losing Stephan. Locked in the crate that stood in the corner of her studio.

She shook now as she opened her paints and mixed them on the palette. She was elated to feel passion flowing through her hands again. And she was terrified that it was Marc Ryder who had opened the floodgate.

CHAPTER FOURTEEN

Ryder urged Wind Walker faster, taking another jump on the cross-country course. Gallop, gallop, gallop, gather, jump. The impact of their landing stung, but the pain was manageable. Her leg was growing stronger every day. Gallop, gallop, gallop, gather, jump. They skirted the really difficult obstacles because the Arabian wasn't bred for jumping, but they had pounded around the center's trails and now the course for much of the afternoon.

She had begun to ride the day after she woke alone in Eleanor's house. She needed to test her limits again and fill her mind with something other than a blond-haired artist.

She had found Bridgette's phone number in the center's office and had left several messages before Bridgette finally returned her call. The woman she spoke to on the phone, however, wasn't the one she'd made love to in the empty mansion, the one who had surprised Ryder by laying her own claim again and again. Although Ryder rarely let her sexual partners take charge, giving herself over to Bridgette's desires felt easy and natural.

But that was before. Now, their conversation felt stilted and difficult. Bridgette was preoccupied, barely listening, absently responding to Ryder's offer for the auction and reception to be held at Eleanor's mansion.

The stallion still breathed easily, but sweat had lathered his white coat into a dark gray and Ryder reined him in to a trot.

What had she hoped for? An acknowledgement that something more intimate than sex had transpired in that upstairs bedroom?

She turned Wind Walker toward the barn. He could feel her agitation and danced sideways. She had to work hard to calm him to a cooling walk and to quiet her churning thoughts.

Damn, she felt like a yo-yo. Come here. Go away. I want to hold you. I'm too busy for you. Still, she couldn't help the anticipation that filled her. Tory and Leah were coming over for dinner, and Bridgette had been invited, too.

She took her time bathing sweat from the stallion before returning him to the pasture. She even stood against the fence for a while, watching him roll in the grass to dry his wet coat. It barely left her enough time to shower before dinner. She was being childish, but she didn't want to appear too anxious for Bridgette to arrive. If she came downstairs too soon, she would pace and give herself away. That wouldn't be cool.

❖

"Bridgette said she couldn't make it tonight," Leah said.

"Why not?" Ryder knew she sounded like a pouting child, but the question was out of her mouth before she could stop it.

Jessica walked by, carrying a plate of deviled eggs, and sniffed Ryder. "Mmm. You smell good."

She'd scrubbed, shaved, and even borrowed a bright-blue polo from Skyler that complemented her tan. All dressed up and no woman to impress.

"She's playing ball. We've got a book deadline but she's got time for softball." Leah didn't look any happier than Ryder felt.

"It's for the season championship, babe," Tory said. "The team is depending on her."

"I'm depending on her, too. We have a contract and a deadline."

"I'm sure she's swamped with preparations for the auction," Jessica said as they moved to the dining room. She sat in the chair Ryder pulled out for her since Skyler's hands were full with a large platter of steaks. "Thank you, Ryder. I haven't been to an art auction since I lived in Atlanta with Mom. We got our invitations yesterday. I was surprised to see they're having it at your grandmother's house."

Leah sighed. "I probably should negotiate an extension on our deadline."

Jessica grimaced and rubbed her belly.

"You okay, babe?" Skyler put down the meat and was immediately at Jessica's side.

Jessica pulled Skyler down for a quick peck on the lips. "Fine. My back is just bothering me. The baby's been kicking my kidneys all afternoon."

"I wanted to talk with Bridgette about a few things and give her the keys to the house," Ryder said, still frowning as they all sat and began to pass food around the table.

"Oh, yeah. She said to ask if you could drop the keys off at the art department in the morning," Leah said. "Her friend is flying down from New York tomorrow to establish some base values for your grandmother's artwork."

"I could have met them there." Ryder sawed into her steak, nearly raw and bloody just like she liked it and sort of how she felt right now.

"Friend from New York?" Skyler asked the question that was chewing at Ryder.

"The owner of the galleries that sell Bridgette's paintings," Leah said.

"Galleries?" Jessica asked.

"One in New York and the other in Boston, where Bridgette lived for a while. She said they've been friends since college."

Ryder didn't like the sound of that. An ex-lover? Everybody knew what happened in those college dorms. "I could take the keys over to her loft."

Skyler pointed her fork at her. "Sounds like she'll be busy entertaining company. You're odd woman out."

"Maybe she was hoping to talk them into a threesome." Tory winked at Skyler.

"Now, there's an idea," Skyler said, warming to their usual teasing. "Think she could handle two women?"

"She's probably done it before."

Skyler chewed her steak and made a show of considering Tory's suggestion. She nodded. "Probably so. But—"

Tory waved her fork. "But, with Bridgette being one of the women, I don't know. She's quite a handful."

"Shut up," Ryder growled, sawing viciously at her meat.

"Ow, that's my foot." Tory grimaced, then sweetly smiled at the foot-stomper. "A handful, but not nearly as amazing as you, babe," she said, giving her glaring partner a quick kiss.

Leah accepted the groveling and turned back to Ryder. "You know what I think?"

Ryder looked up cautiously. Leah tended to say exactly what was on her mind, but she apparently was the only one Bridgette had talked to in the past week and she wondered what she knew.

"I think you should stay away from Bridgette."

Jessica looked surprised. "Why would you say that?"

"Uh-oh." Skyler gave Ryder a disapproving look. "What have you done now, brat?"

"Nothing." Ryder scowled.

Everybody looked to Leah for an explanation. She glared at Ryder.

"Bridgette hasn't been the same since we were trying to work in the barn office while your little tête-à-tête with Alex was going on upstairs."

Ryder's cheeks flushed when the attention turned from Leah to her.

"When?" Skyler demanded. "Exactly when did this happen?"

"Yeah, we had a bet on this," Tory said, frowning at Leah. "Why didn't you tell me about it?"

Ryder ignored them and glared back at Leah. "I apologized to her for that when I took her to see Eleanor's paintings."

"I'm not sure what your apology involved, but she hasn't come out of that studio since. I can barely get her to talk to me on the phone, much less nail her down to a time when we can get some work done."

Ryder's heart lifted. She wasn't the only one Bridgette was avoiding. "I thought we were fine when I saw her last. I'll take the keys to her in the morning and talk to her. Did she say what time she'd be there?"

"I told you, she said to just leave them with the department secretary. She'll be in Richmond, picking her friend up from the airport." Leah raised an eyebrow at Ryder. "Doesn't sound like she wants to see you since she asked for you to drop the keys off when she won't be there."

Ryder was about to tell Leah to butt out when Jessica paled and pushed her plate away.

"Sky—"

Skyler jumped up from her chair and knelt next to Jessica to grasp her hand.

"Are you okay?"

"A little queasy. I think I need to lie down for a bit."

"You're not having contractions, are you?" Ryder jumped up, too, and pulled out Jessica's chair as Skyler helped her stand.

"No. This backache has just ruined my appetite."

"Let's get you on the bed and I'll rub your back for you." Skyler's face was etched with concern.

"Sorry to break up the party," Jessica said weakly as Skyler turned her toward the downstairs master bedroom.

"You go lie down." Leah waved for Tory and Ryder to begin clearing the plates. "We'll clean everything up and then come say good night to you before we leave."

Tory and Leah stood at the sink, washing and drying dishes, while Ryder went outside to clean the grill that had cooled as they ate. On her way back inside, she paused in the mudroom. She could hear their low, intense conversation.

"I'm just saying you were a little hard on my buddy. What goes on between her and Bridgette is their business."

"It's my business when it's affecting our work."

"Seems like it's bothering more than your deadline, babe."

"Bridgette is my friend, too. I know I was a little jealous because she got in your pants before I did, but she backed off when she saw what was happening between us. She's a good person."

"Ryder's a good person, too."

Ryder nodded to herself. She could always count on Tory to stick up for her.

"You're the one who said she likes to love 'em and leave 'em," Leah said.

"Yeah, well, Bridgette's sort of easy-come-easy-go, too. She believes in having 'friends with benefits' so I'd say they're a good match."

Leah laughed. "I think your ego is a little bruised because she let you go so easily."

"She knew my heart—and my pants—would only belong to you."

"Sweet-talker."

They were quiet for a moment, only the clink of silverware filtering from the kitchen.

"Something else is going on with Bridgette, Tory. I don't know what it is, but your buddy bird-dogging her just seems to be making it worse. I think Bridgette is trying to brush her off gently, but Ryder knows she needs those paintings for the auction and is taking advantage of that."

"Ryder isn't like that."

"How do you know? You and Skyler haven't seen her in twelve years. People change."

Tory sighed. "I just know, Leah. Underneath all that bravado is a good, solid soul. But I'll talk to her."

Ryder frowned. The artwork couldn't be the problem. Bridgette had believed her when she made it clear that what was between them had nothing to do with Eleanor's paintings. But what *was* between them? Did Bridgette see her as just another friend with benefits?

Leah said Bridgette was trying to brush her off. Had their night in the mansion been a pity fuck because she told Bridgette about her childhood? How could she have mistaken it for something more? Bitter embarrassment gnawed at her insides. Nobody had to tell her twice. She'd been brushed off before and knew how to hit the road. She grabbed the truck keys from the hook by the back door. There were lots of other women, available women. Why waste her time on somebody who didn't want her?

CHAPTER FIFTEEN

R eally, you guys. Just one beer, then I have to go." Bridgette had pitched a no-hitter to win the regular-season champ-ionship and her team wanted to celebrate. She wanted to go home and paint. But they had welcomed her when she landed in town two years ago, and she owed them at least one drink.

The R&R was loud and teeming with patrons as diverse as the establishment's music. The two lesbian ex-marines who owned the place made it clear that they wouldn't tolerate bias within these walls. The crowd came anyway—gay or straight, liberal or conservative, hawk or dove—because of the huge dance floor, the mechanical bull, Foosball, dartboards, pool tables, vintage video games, and the gourmet selection of beer.

Bridgette wove her way to the tables her teammates had commandeered, her locally brewed Howling Dog Ale icy in her hand. She was tired but at the same time energized. Her week had been a frenzy of painting that was going so well, she felt refreshed despite having little sleep. Her rediscovered confidence had carried over to her softball game tonight, and she had pitched a perfect game of blazing fastballs, snapping curves, deceptive risers, and her favorite, sliders.

The team's catcher, Lou, dropped into the seat beside her and set a second Howling Dog in front of her. She started to protest, but she had almost drained the first and the crushed ice dripping down the sides of the second promised to be just as cool on her parched throat.

"Thanks, but this one is absolutely my…damn, Lou." She frowned at the ice-filled Baggie that Lou gripped in her swollen left hand. "Sorry about that."

Lou grinned broadly. "Don't be. It's just a bit bruised from the fastballs you were throwing. Shit, woman. I don't know why you aren't playing professional ball."

Bridgette shook her head. "I just had a good night. I'm not usually that hot. Besides, I'd rather paint."

"Lucky for us," Desiree said, as she settled in Lou's lap for lack of an open seat. "The championship-tournament trophy is ours to lose this year. You've got it on your calendar, right?"

"Hell, yeah. She better have that weekend reserved," Lou declared.

"Fortunately, it's the weekend after the art auction, so it shouldn't be a problem. I'll probably have to miss some practices before then, though. I've got a million things to do for the event." The team's shortstop placed a third Howling Dog in front of her and walked away, ignoring Bridgette's protest.

Lou waggled her beer at her. "Delegate. That's why you're head of the committee."

"Did you talk to Ryder yet?" Desiree asked.

"About what?" Bridgette spoke before she realized the question was meant for Lou.

"I was going to see if we could add her to the roster for the tournament, if she's still in town," Lou said. She and Desiree clanked their beers together in celebration of what they obviously thought was an excellent idea.

"But we've got a full roster." Bridgette frowned. "What position would she play?"

"Doesn't matter," Lou said smugly. "She can play any position, but what we want is her bat. She holds the Cherokee Falls record for the most home runs in a season. Hell, for the most in one game."

"Yeah. She hit four the night we played the R&R's team," Desiree said. "Can you believe it? Four. The idiot pitcher was so mad, she refused to intentionally walk her."

Lou chuckled. "Ryder paid for it later. Sherry kicked her out of the bar when the team came here to celebrate afterward."

"Sherry kicked her out because she was only seventeen," Desiree said.

When the left fielder plopped a fourth Howling Dog in front of Bridgette, she shoved it toward Lou. "Three is my limit. I have to go." She stood and swayed a little.

Desiree's hand on her arm steadied her. "I think you need to stay a little longer. We've ordered a couple of pizzas for the team, and you look like you need to eat something before you drive home."

Desiree was right. She had been so caught up in painting that she'd eaten nothing all day. "I mean I have to go...literally. I hope the line to the bathroom isn't too long." She squeezed Desiree's hand. "Pizza sounds good. Save my seat for me."

Her head swam a little from exhaustion and beer, so she concentrated on putting one foot before the other. That's why she didn't see the two women until she stumbled into them as she came out of the restroom. Ryder was sandwiched between the wall and one of the blond twins from the team they'd just defeated. The woman had her hands on Ryder's breasts and her tongue in Ryder's mouth.

Ryder pushed the woman back and made a diving catch to stop Bridgette's fall, but they ended up on the floor, Ryder on her back with Bridgette sprawled on top of her.

"Well, if it isn't Moses come down from the mountain. I mean, out of her art cave." Ryder's eyes were hazy and her speech slurred.

"I'm sorry. I didn't see you." She tried to push up from the floor, but Ryder held her fast.

"Let me buy you a drink, gorgeous."

"No, thanks. You appear to be otherwise engaged." She hated the surge of jealousy that burned through her and the instant throbbing in her sex at the feel of Ryder's body under hers.

Ryder grinned. "I'm not engaged. I was just waiting in line for the bathroom and Lisa stopped by to say hello."

Ryder's arms relaxed and she broke free to stand. The blonde had disappeared into the restroom. "That looked like more than a hello, but that's none of my business."

She looked down at Ryder still lying on the floor but didn't offer a hand to help her up. She felt dizzy. Was it the beer still or the overwhelming desire to drag Ryder into a dark corner and kiss her senseless? But the memory of the other woman's hands on Ryder's breasts, her body pressed against Ryder's, soured her impulse. "My dinner's getting cold," she said, and turned to push through the crowd.

Her elation from the game and her appetite were gone, but she forced down the slice of pizza Lou handed her. She felt the heat of Ryder's stare but refused to look toward the table near the mechanical bull where she sat with the twins and other members of the opposing team.

She glanced at her watch. Her earlier need to go home to paint had fled with her appetite, and exhaustion settled over her like a heavy blanket. She needed to sleep. She had to pick Lydia up from the airport in Richmond very early. Shit. She also needed the keys to Eleanor White's house. She had no choice but to speak to Ryder again before she could leave. She both loathed and relished the anticipation that stirred in her.

Suck it up, LeRoy. The woman is making a huge contribution to the auction.

She glanced across the room. Ryder's friends were pointing toward the mechanical bull and Ryder was shaking her head, resisting their entreaties. But they were persistent, grabbing her arm and urging her to stand up. Ryder shook her head again. Then one husky woman slapped a twenty-dollar bill on the table, and Ryder raised an eyebrow. The woman pointed to herself, then Ryder, then the bull.

Her anger flared. Why did they encourage her? Were they too stupid to realize how suicidal it was to play with bulls? Even a mechanical bull was dangerous. She would put a stop to this.

Ryder looked up as she approached.

"Can I talk to you for a minute?"

Ryder stood. Her tablemates protested, but she ignored them and cupped Bridgette's elbow to lead her away. Before Bridgette realized where they were going, she was corralled in a dim corner by an unoccupied pool table. Her back was pressed against the black-painted wall, Ryder's hands planted on either side of her shoulders. Ryder's face was inches from hers, and her skin heated at the naked desire in Ryder's dark eyes, the same desire she remembered from their lovemaking—not tryst—in the mansion the week before.

"I was hoping you would reconsider." Ryder's voice was husky, her speech still slurred. The ale on Ryder's breath mixed with her spicy scent, and Bridgette pushed down the urge to taste those full lips that hovered so close to hers. If she did, she'd be lost. The lazy thump of Ryder's heart reverberated through her as she put her hand on Ryder's chest to gently push her back.

"My art broker is flying in tomorrow morning and I need the keys to your grandmother's house so we can price the paintings."

Ryder pressed heavily against her hand, resisting her effort to create more space between them. "I think I have them in one of my pockets." Her eyes lit up as if she suddenly had a great idea. "You have my permission to search for them."

A roar of cheers rose up from a crowd that was gathering around the mechanical bull. The woman who'd put the twenty on the table was hanging on as the operator twisted and spun the controls to buck her off.

"You're not going to get on that thing, are you? They're nearly as dangerous as a live bull."

"Nah. It's like riding a tricycle compared to a real bull. Not dangerous at all if you know what you're doing."

She frowned. "Don't be stupid. Just last week, you were using a cane to walk. You'll injure your leg again."

Ryder pressed closer. "I can think of something better to do with my time."

"Marc." She couldn't do this. Wouldn't do this. Each kiss, each touch from Ryder's hands made her want more. It was a dangerous addiction, more perilous than Ryder's absurd inclination to risk her neck riding angry bovine.

"I can't stop thinking about last week—how beautiful you are naked." Ryder's gaze was soft and hazy, lost in her reminiscence. The tip of her tongue snaked across her lips. "All I have to do is think about it and I can taste you in my mouth."

She pushed hard with both hands now, catching Ryder off guard so that she stumbled back a few steps. "Stop. All I need from you are the keys to Eleanor's house. Do you have them or not?"

Ryder's expression hardened. "They're outside." She drew the keys to her truck out of her pocket. "It's the blue truck with the equestrian center's logo on it. Look on the seat." She tossed the keys at Bridgette.

"I'll bring these back in a minute."

"Just leave them at the bar with Sherry." Ryder turned away, and she watched her walk back to her friends and quickly down two shots of tequila from a tray the waitress had just delivered to their table.

Christ. She didn't need this kind of drama in her life. Her emotions felt raw and her stomach hollow, despite the pizza she had eaten. She rubbed a hand over her face. She was tired. That's all. Get the keys, get some sleep, and have a great visit with Lydia tomorrow.

When she returned from the parking lot to leave the truck keys at the bar, the shouting almost deafened her. Most of the tables were vacant and the dance floor empty as everyone crowded around the mechanical bull. Ryder was astride it, one arm raised high overhead for balance and her legs pumping to rake her heels along the leather hide as it bucked and twirled crazily.

"Idiot," Bridgette muttered.

"She is one crazy muther," Sherry said, taking the keys. "But she's got more guts than a slaughterhouse."

The mechanism slowed and Ryder hopped up to stand on it and take a bow amid catcalls and whistles. She swayed, then caught her balance, grinned and bowed again. She was about to jump down when the bull bucked and whirled, flinging Ryder head over heels beyond the floor padding and into the nearest table.

Before Bridgette had time to think, she was kneeling next to Ryder, who groaned and rolled onto her back. She froze. Blood, red and bright, streamed from Ryder's nose, covering her cheeks and dripping from her chin to soak into her shirt.

"Oh, man, I am so sorry." Sherry's partner and co-owner, Jo-Jo, knelt next to Bridgette. "I was reaching for my beer and my elbow accidently hit the controls. You okay?"

"I'm dandy. I've got so much tequila in me, it didn't really hurt." Ryder sat up, her bloody grin a macabre contradiction to her words. "I think I need to work on my back flip, though. Want to try that again?"

The careless words burned through Bridgette like a fury, and she slapped Ryder so hard the crowd jumped back to avoid the blood spray.

Ryder frowned. "Ow. Now that did hurt. What'd ya slug me for?"

"Trying to knock some sense into you," she said through clenched teeth. "Get up. I'm going to drive you to the emergency room."

"I don't need a doctor, just maybe another shot of Jose."

"Your nose could be broken."

"I've broken my nose before. This doesn't feel broken."

"I don't think you're feeling much of anything right now," Jo-Jo interjected. "Maybe you should listen to Bridgette and go get it checked out. I don't want you suing me next week because it is broke and you've started snoring so bad no woman will sleep with you."

"I'll stop by Tory's and get her to look at it."

Bridgette huffed. "Tory is a veterinarian, not a doctor. But then you are acting like an ass."

Jo-Jo laughed and Ryder glared at her. "Shut up and help me get up."

She struggled to her feet with Jo-Jo and Bridgette's help, but her face paled. She closed her eyes and swallowed hard. "I don't feel so good now," she muttered.

Bridgette guided Ryder to a chair. "Watch her. I'll be right back."

She returned with two clean towels, dampened with ice water. She pressed one against the back of Ryder's neck and gently cleaned her bloody face with the other. Her nose wasn't swelling too badly, but Ryder's eyes were unfocused and clouded with more than alcohol.

"Help me get her in my car, Jo-Jo. She's going to see a doctor whether she wants to or not."

Ryder didn't protest this time as Jo-Jo shouldered under her arm, held her tight around the waist, and shuffled toward the parking lot.

"She okay?" Lou asked.

"I'm going to make sure," she said, handing her the bloody towels. "Can you get Marc's keys from Sherry and have someone drive her truck back to Skyler's place?"

"Sure. Desiree and I'll take care of it." Lou wrapped her big hand around Bridgette's forearm and gave it a squeeze. "Don't be too hard on her, Bridgette. Showing off and doing crazy things is just Ryder. That's who she is."

She nodded, but she didn't really agree. She was beginning to understand that it was just who Ryder was pretending to be.

Chapter Sixteen

R yder was afraid that if she opened her eyes, the warm fingers gently clasping her cold hand would withdraw.

Her knee was stiff, but a quick X-ray and examination revealed only a little swelling of the soft tissue. The metal plate and pins holding her newly mended shin together were intact. And while her nose was swollen enough that she had to breathe through her mouth, the cartilage was not broken.

The nausea and pounding in her head, however, were keeping her in the emergency room, now going on four hours. She shivered at the caress of Bridgette's thumb against the back of her hand.

"Are you cold? I can ask for another blanket."

She tightened her fingers around Bridgette's to stop her from pulling free.

"This stupid gown doesn't cover much, but I don't want to get too comfortable. I'd rather dress and get out of here. What's taking that doctor so long?"

"He's waiting on your MRI results."

"You don't have to stay. I know you have to get up early." Even as she said it, she clung to Bridgette's hand, pathetically unable to let go.

"How do you think you'll get home?"

"I can call Skyler or Tory."

"I'm fine. I'm not going to leave you here alone."

She sighed. She'd always been alone. That's why she filled her life with distractions—beautiful women, exciting places, and adrenaline-pumping experiences.

Then she met Bridgette. Something about her made Ryder feel the loneliness again. Made her feel everything.

She'd been embarrassed when giving her medical history. She couldn't answer the routine questions about heart disease or cancer in her family. She had to explain that, yes, her parents were alive, but, no, she didn't know exactly where they were currently living. They were probably still in South Africa.

She usually told people her parents were dead. But Bridgette already knew about them and she didn't want to lie in front of her, no matter how ashamed she was that she knew so little about them.

"Maybe it won't be much longer." She was torn between guilt and need. She needed, wanted desperately for Bridgette to stay close. But she felt guilty that her antics were responsible for keeping her from going home and getting some sleep.

They had barely made it out of the bar when she'd pushed away from Jo-Jo and stumbled over to empty her stomach in the shrubbery. It wasn't the alcohol. She'd consumed a lot more tequila before and never lost her dinner.

She didn't need a doctor to diagnose her, either. The symptoms were familiar—slightly blurred vision, sensitivity to light, nausea, and a pounding headache. She'd had a lot of concussions during her riding career. Enough to know that a couple days of rest and a handful of pain pills were the only cure.

She was about to ask Bridgette to help her put her pants on when the doctor stepped around the curtain.

"Well, Ms. Ryder. Your MRI scan doesn't show any swelling or lesions, but your symptoms indicate a mild concussion." He gave Ryder a disapproving look. "We can't be sure, however, because your blood-alcohol level also could be responsible for your slurred speech when you arrived in the ER and your nausea and your headache now."

"Fine. Can I go now?"

"I'm not finished. Your medical history indicates you are an athlete and have experienced multiple concussions since you were a teen. Are you aware that new studies indicate cumulative damage from multiple concussions can cause significant neurological and emotional problems?"

"Yeah, I've seen the publicity about pro football players having brain damage."

"Then I shouldn't have to caution you further. You know the risks."

"Yeah, okay." The lights were too bright and her head hurt. She just wanted to go home.

"I understand you are recovering from recent orthopedic injury. I would caution you against taking any anti-inflammatory prescriptions you may have over the next couple of days because of the risk of intracranial bleeding. You can, however, take acetaminophen for pain."

She started to nod, which only caused a new wave of nausea. "I know the drill. I'll pick up some on the way home."

The doctor handed Bridgette a sheet with instructions. "She shouldn't drive and someone should keep an eye on her for the next twenty-four to forty-eight hours. There's a drugstore across town that stays open all night, or you can take a left at the nurses' desk, go to the end of the hall, and take a right. The hospital pharmacy is open."

"Thank you, Doctor." Bridgette took the instructions.

"You can dress, but wait here until the nurse comes back. She'll give you an injection that will help with the nausea."

Bridgette watched him leave. "Ready to get dressed?"

Ryder moved slowly. She would have given a hundred bucks for a pair of sunglasses to block the light that was piercing her brain, but she was determined not to dry heave again in front of Bridgette. She was sweating and shaking by the time they got her clothes on, and she sat on the bed so Bridgette could gently put her boots on for her.

"Maybe this little accident wasn't such a bad thing after all."

Ryder lay back and covered her eyes to gather her strength. "You can say that. Your brain isn't trying to pound its way out of your skull," she muttered.

"I hope you listen to him and start thinking about a different career."

"Ain't gonna happen." She didn't want to think about anything while this jackhammer was going off in her head.

"I think your brain is already scrambled. Or maybe you're just hoping to break your neck and get it over with quickly."

The venom in Bridgette's voice startled her.

"I wear safety gear, Bridgette." She sat up a little too quick and her stomach roiled. When she looked frantically around the room, Bridgette tossed the puke basin into her lap.

"I'll go get your medicine."

❖

Of all the moronic egomaniacs, why did she get saddled with this one? Bridgette was furious.

She suddenly realized she had always blamed herself in some small way for her brother's death. She should have guessed what he was up to and insisted that he watch with her from the balcony. But now she knew no amount of logic would have dissuaded him. And that made her furious.

How could Stephan and Ryder be so careless with their lives, with the feelings of the people who cared about them? She stopped in the middle of the hallway. She didn't care about Ryder. She'd just met her. She was an arrogant, mule-headed, macho prick. Bridgette sighed. She was sexy and charming and sweet and passionate.

A shiver ran through her. Though Ryder was an incredible lover, it was the vulnerable woman she'd only glimpsed that touched her deep inside, made her want to heal and protect. But how could she take on someone else's baggage when she couldn't even deal with her own issues? Ryder was just like Stephan. His insane recklessness had both thrilled and terrified her. Still, she'd let herself love him and look how that turned out.

She started walking again, then realized she must have taken a wrong turn. Why did hospitals have to be a maze of hallways? Every hallway looked the same, but nothing looked familiar. There had to be a nurses' station around here somewhere.

She was about to backtrack when a familiar figure brought her up short.

Skyler was leaning against the wall and talking on her cell phone.

"No, just a false alarm, Laura. She's fine. The baby's fine. I'd feel better, though, if you and Kate would fly back to the States pretty soon. Dr. Nichols says it won't be long." Skyler looked up at her. "Thanks. Okay, I'll tell her. We love you guys, too." She ended the call and smiled at Bridgette.

"Is Jess okay?"

"Yeah. False labor. They're sending her back home." Skyler looked harried but happy. She raked her long fingers through her shaggy blond hair. "Damn, I need to get a haircut before the baby comes. What are you doing up here? Did someone get hurt at the game? Did you guys win?"

She had forgotten that she was still dressed for softball, except for the tennis shoes that had replaced her cleats.

"The only thing hurt was the other team's egos," she said quickly, then grinned. "I pitched my first real no-hitter tonight."

"No shit? Congratulations. So, you up here to see a friend?"

She frowned as her earlier irritation resurfaced. "Actually, one of *your* friends had an accident at the R&R and I drove her to the ER."

Most on Bridgette's team were women Skyler had grown up with in Cherokee Falls. "Which one?"

"Marc."

"Ryder? We wondered where she'd gone off to. She okay? Did she hurt her leg?"

"Her leg is fine, but her stupidly hard head was injured."

Skyler laughed. "Well, if she fell on her head, she should be okay."

Damn it. Was she the only one who recognized how dangerous this could be? "Have you ever had a concussion?" Her scowl must have clued Skyler that she wasn't amused, because she stopped laughing.

"Yeah, a couple of times when I was working as a professional rider. Sometimes you were hired to ride a horse only once or twice, so you didn't get a chance to know it. That always increases the possibility of misreading the cues and taking a tumble."

"You still jump horses." Bridgette's tone was accusing, but Skyler didn't take the bait.

"I do, but I spend most of my time giving lessons and working with the kids now. When I do jump horses, as a trainer, I've had plenty of opportunity to get to know the horse before I take it over the jumps." Skyler glanced toward the hospital-room door next to them. "I have to be more careful now that I've got other people depending on me."

"So, I guess if you're single, it's okay to act like a twenty-eight-year-old juvenile, foolishly taking idiotic chances with your life. What if Marc broke her neck riding those bulls and was paralyzed? Or worse, killed? Does she think nobody would care?"

"Uh—"

A nurse rolled a wheelchair up to Skyler, oblivious to the argument she was interrupting. "I'm sure we'll see you soon, but you can go ahead and take her home tonight."

"Thanks," Skyler said, taking charge of the chair and looking relieved. "Jess is ready. She's really disappointed it's not happening tonight, though." She turned back to Bridgette. "You want to come in and say hey?"

She looked at her watch. "No. Marc's waiting for me to give her a ride home. I was just looking for the pharmacy to pick up some acetaminophen for her."

"We've got plenty at home. If you like, she can go with us since we're on our way out."

"I do have to get up early. That would be great."

"No problem."

"I didn't mean to go off on you." She let out a frustrated breath. "I just get so aggravated with her." She gave Skyler's hand a squeeze. "Take care of Jess. Hopefully, I'll see you two at the auction, if not before." She started to walk away but turned back. "Oh. They were supposed to give her a shot for nausea while I went to the pharmacy. But she's been throwing up a lot, so you may want to leave the window down, too, when you drive her home."

Bridgette walked briskly to the parking lot without stopping in the ER, where Ryder lay wounded and hurting. Part of her wanted to take Ryder to her loft, to watch over her, to wipe her brow and rub her back while she threw up. A bigger part wanted to run far enough away that she could forget those dark eyes and that dangerous grin.

Retching over the puke basin had pushed her headache from bad to worse, so Ryder paid little attention when the attractive nurse exposed a lot more of her butt than necessary, took a lot longer than usual to administer the injection, and then slipped her phone number into Ryder's pocket before she left. Instead, she closed her eyes and sank into the blissful drowsiness the medicine induced.

Her last thought was of Bridgette as the sounds of the hospital receded.

She couldn't really recall what she'd said to make her so mad, but when Bridgette returned, she planned to beg to spend the night at the loft, and hopefully she'd feel well enough to talk it out in the morning. It wasn't a surefire plan, but it was the best her muddled brain could come up with and she felt reasonably hopeful, right up until the moment Skyler shook her awake.

"Damn, what happened to your nose? No wonder you were snoring like a freight train."

"What? What are you doing here? Where's Bridgette?"

"Gone home. She said she has to get up early."

Ryder sat up carefully. Her head was fuzzy, but the pounding was only a dull ache and her stomach had settled. "Did she call you?"

"No. I ran into her down the hall. I told her you could ride with us since we were already here."

Everything jumped into sharp focus as she recalled Jessica feeling sick at dinner. "Jess, the baby. Is something wrong?"

"I'm fine. Just false labor pains." Jessica was sitting in a wheelchair slightly behind Skyler, looking up at her with concern. "What happened to you?"

She gingerly felt her nose and wondered how bad it looked. Why did things always go haywire when Bridgette was around? "I was standing on the mechanical bull at R&R and Jo-Jo accidently elbowed the controls."

"What the hell were you doing standing on it?"

Ryder blinked at Skyler, realizing how stupid she sounded. "Don't remember, exactly," she lied.

Skyler shook her head. "Can you walk or should I go find another a wheelchair and somebody to help us?"

"I can walk." Ryder slowly stood. She still felt fuzzy, but after a slight wave of dizziness she found her balance.

"Why don't you wheel me out while Skyler pulls the car up?" Jessica suggested. "It might help to hold onto the wheelchair."

Skyler watched while Ryder gripped the handles and turned the chair toward the door. "You good?" she asked.

"Yeah, we'll meet you outside."

A quick kiss on Jessica's cheek and Skyler was gone.

Ryder wheeled Jessica carefully out of the ER to the curb and squatted next to the chair. "You warm enough?"

"I'm fine. This baby is like carrying around a furnace. The night air feels good." Jessica looked at her with affection. "You're sweet to ask, though."

She sat on the curb and pulled her legs up to rest her chin on her knees. She was very, very tired.

"It's a beautiful night, don't you think?"

She shrugged. It seemed bleak to her.

"Skyler said Bridgette was upset with you. Is that what you're worried about?"

Over the weeks that they had exercised together each day, they had become friends. Jessica was a good listener. They would walk laps back and forth in the pool for nearly an hour before Ryder realized Jessica's gentle questions had coaxed her into revealing more of herself than she'd shared with most. She was wary of that tonight, because she felt abandoned. It was a festering wound that hadn't bled since she had changed her name and left town to put the pathetic Marci Ridenhouer behind her.

"She didn't even stop by to tell me she was going." She turned her head away so Jessica couldn't see the tears welling in her eyes. Marci Ridenhouer might cry, but Marc Ryder didn't. She swallowed the tightness in her throat.

"You were probably asleep and she didn't want to wake you." Jessica's hand was warm on her shoulder. "We can talk about it when you're feeling better, if you want."

She nodded, relieved that Jessica wasn't going to pry. There was nothing to talk about. Not tonight. Not tomorrow. Bridgette had said she wouldn't leave her, but she did.

"I got blood all over Skyler's shirt," she said, to change the subject.

Jessica patted her shoulder. "Don't worry about it. She has a drawer full of those shirts. Besides, it'll come out in the wash."

She rested her head on her knees and felt like whatever it was that kept people from caring about her was a stain that would never wash out.

CHAPTER SEVENTEEN

"We're never going to get this done in time. We need help. You've unearthed a treasure chest." Lydia pulled painting after painting from the racks and lined them up against the wall. "It's true some of them are unfinished or just crap, but there must be at least fifty well worth auctioning."

They had already spent three days sorting and appraising the paintings that hung downstairs before Bridgette had led Lydia upstairs to the studio. It was easier to come up with prices on Eleanor's collection of other artists because they could compare each painting to that artist's history of sales. But these Eleanor White canvases had never been circulated before.

"I have no idea how to price them," Bridgette admitted.

"I think we should sort them into four groups, setting the base price for the least valuable at ten thousand and the most valuable at fifty thousand."

"You don't think that's too much?"

"God, no. You'll get way more than that. It's just a starting point for the auctioneer. But if you don't sell all of them, I can find buyers after the auction. Just the fact that she's dead and they've never been on the market before increases their value."

"It's a pity artists have to die before they're really respected," Bridgette said absently.

"I'd rather have several opinions before I price them, but you haven't given me much time. I do have a friend who used to appraise for Sotheby's. I can probably get him down here on short notice."

"We don't have much of a budget to work with, and we're using most of it for down payments on the catering and the like. Would he be willing to wait until after the auction to get paid?"

"I can guarantee it." Lydia held up a large canvas that depicted a field of wildflowers. In the distance, a pensive, dark-haired child sat on a large rock, small and alone among the riot of color. "I can't believe her granddaughter is donating all of the paintings. This one is amazing."

"I think she plans to sell the house. She's visiting here for several months, but she lives in Dallas."

"This is an incredibly generous donation. You must have slept with her or promised your firstborn."

Bridgette's cheeks flushed as she turned away and picked up a canvas, pretending to study it. But she didn't fool Lydia.

"Slut! You did sleep with her. What's she like? Is she as beautiful and creative as Eleanor was?"

"No. She's a twenty-eight-year-old juvenile with a stupidly hard head, who takes foolishly idiotic chances."

Bridgette whirled toward the husky voice. Ryder was slouched against the doorframe. Despite the purple bruise across the bridge of her nose, she looked lethally sexy in black jeans and a black button-down shirt with the cuffs rolled back off her wrists.

"Isn't that how you described me to Skyler?"

"I was angry with you for being careless with yourself." The throbbing of her pulse wasn't from anger now, but she'd never admit it to Ryder. Especially not in front of Lydia. "Have you thought about what the doctor said?"

Ryder shrugged. "I thought about it. Then I forgot it. Just like *you* forgot me."

Her tone and smile bordered on teasing, as though she was accusing Bridgette of leaving her at the mall rather than injured in a hospital bed. But her eyes said it was more.

"I didn't forget you. I had to get up early and Skyler offered to take you home. Since you're staying with them, it didn't make sense for me to drive you all the way out there."

The air between them was thick with tension as they stared each other down. Ryder looked away first, pushing off the doorframe and turning to Lydia, who was watching them carefully. She extended her hand. "I'm Marc Ryder, Eleanor's granddaughter."

Lydia slid her slender hand into Ryder's. "Lydia Wells. I'm very pleased to meet you," she said. She cocked her head, then turned the painting she had propped against her leg toward Ryder. "You must be the child in this painting."

Ryder shrugged. "Looks like it. I haven't seen that one before."

"You may wish to keep it then."

"No. You can sell it with the rest."

"That's very generous, Ms. Ryder."

"My friends just call me Ryder."

"Then I'd love to count myself among your friends...Ryder."

Bridgette had seen Lydia work a seduction before and it usually amused her. This time, it made her grind her teeth. She picked up a painting and shoved it at her. "Where should I put this one?"

Lydia took the painting but kept her eyes on Ryder. "If you're free tonight, we could become better friends over dinner."

Ryder kissed the back of Lydia's hand. "I would be flattered, but perhaps another time. I've already promised to sit with a very pregnant friend while her partner attends a board meeting tonight."

"I suppose you already have a date for the auction, too?"

"I'm afraid I do." Ryder turned to Bridgette. "I know you're busy, but I need a word with you."

Bridgette hesitated. She wasn't sure she wanted to be alone with Ryder, but she certainly didn't want to discuss anything personal in front of Lydia. "I'll walk you out," she said.

She was surprised that Ryder kept her distance as they stepped into the living room, fishing a folded paper out of her pocket and handing it over.

"I wrote down the contact for the cleaning company. They'll take care of whatever you need, even moving furniture for the auction. They'll also clean up afterward." Ryder held up a hand to stop her protest. "It's a tax deduction."

"Thank you." She had braced for angry words. She wasn't prepared for Ryder's all-business conversation. "I'm sorry about Lydia. She's rather direct."

"No harm." Ryder looked like she wanted to say more, then looked away and continued explaining the contents of the paper.

"The second contact is my attorney. He'll prepare an agreement transferring ownership of the paintings you select and requesting that the endowment be named after Eleanor. She would have liked that."

"Of course. I'm sure the board would be happy to comply with that stipulation."

"The third number is my real-estate agent's. If you would please notify her when you have cleared everything from the house that is sold at the auction, she'll wait until then to list the property for sale. You can turn the house keys over to her."

"So you are selling the house?"

"Yes. In fact, I don't know how much longer I'll be in town. I promised Skyler I'd stay until the baby is born, but I don't think Jess will hold out much longer. The auction is still two weeks away and I may be gone by then."

She stared at Ryder. "You're going back to Dallas," she stated.

"Yes. That's where I live."

"I thought we had a date for the auction."

"We still do if Jess doesn't have the baby before then. If she does, then I'm afraid I'll have to bow out."

Damn her. "You have a concussion. Your face is still black and blue."

"The rodeo-association doctor will have to clear me physically before I can enter events again."

Her anger rose, quick and hot. "Do you think they care if you scramble your brains or some bull stomps you in the dirt again?" Her volume increased with each word and she was aware that Lydia had appeared at the top of the stairs, listening.

Ryder raised a nonchalant eyebrow, her response calm. "Sure, they care. They have to protect their asses against lawsuits." She walked away, a clear signal that their conversation was over. But when she put her hand on the door, she turned back.

"What I don't understand is why it matters to you." Ryder didn't wait for her to answer.

"I don't know," Bridgette whispered to the closed door.

❖

Ryder was just pulling into the equestrian center's drive when her cell phone rang and she checked the caller. Ross Johnston, her agent.

"Yeah?"

"That article on you in the ESPN magazine has generated a lot of interest. When are you coming back to work?"

It was all about business for Ross, but Ryder appreciated that. She didn't care to make small talk with him. Unlike Hollywood portrayals of stars and their agents, Ross was not her friend. They didn't even like each other. He believed riding bulls was men's work. But he was an excellent contract negotiator and knew how to make money from the novelty of a woman competing in a man's sport.

"My leg is good. I've been riding, even jumping a bit. It's sooner than they expected, but I think I can get cleared to compete."

"I'll make that appointment for you and call back."

"You don't think they'll feel it's too soon?" She wanted, needed to get back to work.

"I can take care of that. You've got plenty of personal insurance. I'll draw up a waiver clearing them of any liability if you are re-injured."

"You're all heart." Her tone was sarcastic, but she welcomed his lack of concern for her welfare. She didn't want people to care about her, because then *she* would start to care, to need them. That's when she'd find out they didn't care enough.

"You don't pay me to hold your hand."

"True. I pay you to find me sponsors."

"Your sponsors are very happy about the ESPN article and want to see you qualify for the national."

"Then I need to be back within the month. I promised to stay until my friend has her baby, but that should be any day now. Go ahead and see if you can get me an appointment with the doc in a couple of weeks. That should be plenty of time."

"I'll see if they have an opening and e-mail you the details. Baby or not, you better show up."

"Don't I always?"

She apparently had already disappointed everyone else in her life. Why not Jessica and Skyler, too?

Chapter Eighteen

Ryder opened the e-mail from Ross, confirming the details of her appointment with the rodeo-association's doctor. Jessica had better pop that baby out soon or Skyler would just have to understand. After all, this was business, right?

She'd avoided going into town over the past week. She didn't want to run into Bridgette in the coffee shop or the R&R again. But her grandmother's house had drawn her like a siren because she knew Bridgette was there. She pictured her in Eleanor's studio, the blond highlights of her curly mane glinting like spun gold under the sunlight streaming from the large windows. Her long fingers tracing the figures on a canvas, her full lips pressed tightly together as she considered the painting's worth.

When the urge became too strong to resist, she had saddled Wind Walker and taken a circuitous route through the state park to emerge behind the stables of the mansion. She told herself she needed the long ride to strengthen her leg, but it was really because she didn't want to drive past, in case Bridgette saw the truck and realized she was hanging about like a love-sick teenager.

She had skirted the stables, staying hidden along the edges of the woods and watching as cars and trucks came and went to unload staging lights and decorations in preparation for the event.

She had caught only a glimpse of Bridgette, stepping out the front door to greet Lydia and a gray-haired man. Lydia had touched Bridgette's shoulder and trailed her fingers down Bridgette's arm to clasp her hand with a familiarity that rankled Ryder. She remembered

Lydia's hand in hers. It was smooth and elegant, but generated none of the heat, the electricity she felt when she held Bridgette's.

Shaking herself from her thoughts, she printed her agent's e-mail to tuck in her luggage. She had already packed, dressing each day out of her suitcase so she'd be ready the moment she could put Cherokee Falls behind her again.

She found Jessica in the den, sitting on the sofa with a book at her side and rubbing her swollen belly. Skyler was gone for the day, supervising her young equestrians at a daylong show and leaving Ryder on baby-watch. Tory and Leah had gone with her as backup if Jessica went into labor and Skyler had to hightail it back.

"Everything okay? Can I get you anything?"

Jessica sighed. "Get this baby out of my stomach. She's really restless today and being a pain in the belly."

"You're having pains?"

Jessica chuckled. "You and Skyler both look like you're going to faint every time I say something like that. I'm not in labor." She leaned forward and rubbed at her lower back. "But I would like to take a walk in the pool. It might help my backache."

She helped Jessica stand. "Your lifeguard is at your service, ma'am."

Jessica squeezed her hand. "It's been wonderful having you here. I can't tell you how much Skyler appreciates it, even if it did take an awful accident to get you to come home."

She nodded but didn't reply. She hovered at Jessica's side as they went outside and settled into the golf cart for the short ride to the gymnasium.

"This is your home," Jessica said softly. "Please promise you'll come back often to visit. We'd love for you to spend Christmas with us."

"I'll try," she said, but knew she wouldn't. It'd probably be another twelve years before she returned, if ever. She loved her friends, but they were a constant reminder of what she was missing in her life.

The show Skyler had gone to was a big annual event in the next county, so most of the center's clients were there, too. That meant she and Jessica had the gym and pool to themselves.

Jessica grabbed her swimsuit from the locker and sat on the wood bench nearby. "I'll just change out here."

Skyler, protective and a bit possessive with her pregnant partner, usually showed up to take Jessica into one of the small dressing stalls to help her. But Ryder didn't mind Jessica's lack of modesty. They were both athletes and had changed in front of other women many times in gyms or cramped, makeshift dressing rooms at horse shows.

"Do you need help?"

"I think I can manage," Jessica said, frowning and rubbing her belly again.

Ryder politely turned away to her own locker and began to strip off her jeans.

"Oh. Uh-oh."

Something in Jessica's voice made Ryder whirl around. She was still dressed, sitting on the bench. But her legs were spread wide to avoid putting her feet in the pool of fluid on the floor in front of her. She looked up.

"I think my water just broke."

Ryder froze for a second, then jumped into action. "Holy crap. The baby's coming. I'll go get the truck." She yanked her jeans up and fumbled in her locker. "Where did I put the damn keys?"

"We drove the golf cart, remember? The truck keys are at the house."

"Oh, yeah. Right." She grabbed Jessica's arm to pull her up. "Skyler. We have to call Skyler. I didn't bring my cell phone."

"Wait. Ryder, wait."

"We have to go. We need to get to the hospital."

"I need you to get a couple of towels for me."

"Oh, no. I can deliver baby horses but not baby people. I'll pass out. I know I will."

"Calm down, Miss I-don't-know-nuthin'-about-birthin'-no-babies. My pants are soaked and I don't want to mess up the seat on the golf cart."

"Oh. Right." She raced to the closet then back with an armload of thick white towels. She threw several on the slippery floor and helped Jessica stand. They walked slowly out to the golf cart where Ryder laid the towels out for Jessica to sit on and then drove carefully back to the house. The first contraction hit as Ryder helped her up the steps.

"Tell me what to do, Jess. Do I need to call an ambulance?"

"Heavens, no. Help me inside and I'll call Skyler and the doctor."

It seemed like forever before Jessica was ready for the hospital.

Her suitcase was packed, but she insisted on taking a shower before they left. Ryder helped her undress, then stood by while she showered, afraid to leave her alone for even a minute.

Jessica was beautiful, her pregnant body lush with curves and her skin glowing with a softness that begged to be touched. Helping her prepare for the birth of her baby felt intimate but not sexual, and emotion swelled up in Ryder. She regretted that Skyler wasn't experiencing this moment, this exhilaration of expectation, with her lover.

She was assisting Jessica out of the car at the hospital when Leah's convertible screeched to a stop behind them and Skyler jumped out. Ryder was relieved to see her.

The pains were coming quicker than expected for a maiden delivery. Everything was happening too fast. At least it seemed that way to Ryder. Then two hours later, everything had slowed to a crawl. Skyler and Jessica were settled into a birthing room while Ryder paced the maternity waiting room like an expectant father.

She was alone. It would be evening before Tory and Leah would be done with the show and could come to the hospital. Jessica's parents, Kate and Laura, were in an airplane somewhere over the Atlantic Ocean, returning from their rented villa in Greece. She didn't want to be alone. Every cell in her body longed for Bridgette to be there in the waiting room with her.

She flopped into a chair and cradled her head in her hands as she stared at the floor. She imagined Bridgette as the pregnant woman in the shower and herself as the anxious partner holding a towel up and begging her to hurry.

Damn. Where'd that come from? She'd never even thought about spending the rest of her life with one woman, much less raising children. Hell, she couldn't even commit to sharing her life with a dog. She had raised Wind Walker from a baby and hadn't thought twice about leaving him with Skyler and not returning to see him over the past twelve years. She was truly a chip off the old Ridenhouer block.

❖

Bridgette impatiently laid her checklist on the kitchen counter when the doorbell sounded. She should feel happier. The auction was one week away, but everything was falling into place. Even her own contribution to the auction was finished and currently with the framers.

Still, she felt anxious and unsettled. She blamed it on the pressure for this to be a success, but she knew better. She hated that her heart jumped with expectation every time the door to Eleanor's mansion opened or the doorbell rang. She was irritated that the person she most wanted to see step through the door was Ryder. For what? So she could be reminded that the only thing Ryder cared about was the thrill she got from risking her life?

For the tenth time that day, she brushed Ryder from her thoughts. Obviously, she wouldn't ring the doorbell. It was probably a delivery person, but instead, she found the slender, elderly woman whom she had seen in the gallery with Ryder the day they met.

"Hello. Can I help you with something?"

"Oh, I hope so." The woman held out her hand. "I'm Trudy Wasson, one of Eleanor's neighbors. My grandson is one of your students. Richard Wasson?"

Bridgette clasped her hand briefly and stepped back. "Yes, he is. It's nice to meet you. Would you like to come in?"

"Thank you, dear. I won't keep you long. The neighborhood is buzzing about the auction you're planning, so I know you must have a lot to do other than entertain an old lady."

"Nonsense. I could use a break."

She led Trudy to the living room, where they settled on one of the large sofas. Although professional lighting had been added to properly display the paintings hanging in the downstairs rooms, little of the furniture had been moved because this was where the pre-auction reception would be held. The actual bidding would take place in the huge formal dining room.

Trudy looked around the room. "It hasn't changed much in here," she said. "I feel like Eleanor might barge right in at any moment. She never just walked into a room. It was more like she was leading a charge to take care of some urgent matter."

"You knew Eleanor well?"

"We were neighbors for years. She was a wonderful, talented woman, but she suffered so much from her illness."

"You're referring to her bipolar disorder? Her granddaughter told me about that."

Trudy was about to answer when Lydia came thumping down the stairs.

"Hey, Bridge, look what I found." She stopped in the doorway. "Oh, I'm sorry. I didn't realize someone else was here."

"It's quite all right," Trudy assured them, standing to offer Lydia her hand. "I'm Trudy Wasson."

Lydia set the canvas she carried at her feet and returned Trudy's greeting. "Lydia Wells."

"Trudy is a neighbor and was a friend of Eleanor," Bridgette said.

"Really? Then maybe you can tell me who painted this? I stumbled across another studio upstairs. It doesn't look like Eleanor's work. Did she have a lover who was an artist?"

"Eleanor had a lot of lovers but never kept any around very long. I suspect I know the artist, though. Could I see the room you're talking about?"

"It's upstairs, at the end of the hallway."

Eleanor's studio took up the half of the upstairs area to the right of the staircase, while a long hallway to the left led to a series of bedrooms. Bridgette was aware there was a guest suite on the right before you reached Eleanor's rooms and that Ryder's childhood bedroom, where they'd made love, was first on the left. She had taken for granted that the second door much farther down on the left was another guest bedroom. Instead, it was a small studio.

Sketches, taped nearly from floor to ceiling, were portraits of horses—running, show jumping, looking out of stable doors, or grazing in serene pastures. There were also several portraits of young women, all beautiful. The sketches weren't the work of a professional, but the artist showed a lot of promise. Even the greatest talent required training to reach its potential.

Trudy smiled. "Yes, I thought so. This is Marci's work."

Bridgette gasped. "Marci? These are Marc's sketches?"

"She definitely has some of her grandmother's talent. It's a shame she was never interested in developing it. It was horses, horses, horses from the first time she rode one over at Leigh Parker's place."

Bridgette scanned the wall of sketches. The horses were beautifully drawn. The portraits of girls were less skilled, but one positioned in at the center of the collage of drawings made her pause. She raised her eyebrows. It was a drawing of a young woman reclined on a bed, one hand on her breast and the other between her legs, her head thrown back in ecstasy. This one had definite potential.

Trudy chuckled. "She liked the girls and they liked her, too. Our little Marci was something of a rogue in her teen years."

"This is the one you need to see," Lydia said, drawing their attention to an easel in the corner. She lifted a swath of linen cloth that covered a dark, turbulent abstract so full of passion Bridgette nearly forgot to breathe.

It was good. Very good. The artist's signature in the bottom corner was simply MR.

Several more canvases were stacked against the wall, and she knelt to flip through them. None were as good as the stormy abstract, and several appeared to be attempts at copying the style of well-known masters. One Van Goghish painting was a portrait of Eleanor applying paint to a canvas. Her back was turned to ignore the shadow-like figure of a child kneeling behind her with arms outstretched.

"Oh, my." Trudy dabbed at her eyes. "That one just breaks my heart."

Bridgette suddenly felt as though they were exposing a very private part of Ryder's life, and the callousness of their invasion sliced at her like a razor.

"Most of these are just the drawings of a child," Lydia said, oblivious to their intrusion. "But I'm betting I can get a good price for the abstract."

"No."

Lydia looked surprised. "What do you mean, no? She said we could sell any paintings in the house. She doesn't want them."

"Not this one." Bridgette covered it again.

"At least ask her about it."

"I don't know if she's still in town." She herded them out of the room and closed the door. "After the auction, I'll pack all of this up for her. She might not want it now, but she will someday. I'm sure Skyler will store it for her."

Lydia frowned. "But—"

"It's not up for discussion, Lydia. Don't touch anything in that room."

"Okay. Don't get huffy about it." Lydia disappeared into Eleanor's studio to continue her inventory, and Bridgette led Trudy down the stairs.

"I think I'm going to pour a glass of wine. Would you like some?"

"No, thank you. But I wouldn't mind a glass of water."

Trudy followed her into the kitchen. "You're right, you know. Those are Marci's private things." She shook her head, her eyes sad. "That poor child. Her parents just left her here and took off."

The thought made Bridgette's heart ache. "I can't imagine what that must have felt like. I don't see my parents as much as I'd like, but they were wonderful when my brother and I were growing up."

"Eleanor, bless her heart, was so involved with her art and so consumed by her illness that she wasn't much of a parent either. I wondered sometimes if Marci was afraid she would end up like Eleanor if she became an artist, too."

"Marc told me a little about what it was like living with her."

"I'm afraid it scarred her for life. I came over one Christmas Eve to bring some cookies I'd baked, and Eleanor was locked in her bedroom, having one of her depressions. Little Marci was only eight, so I took her to my house and sent my husband out to buy a list of toys I thought she'd like. We kept her with us so Santa could visit her at our house and she could have a real Christmas dinner. The poor little thing. After that, I always checked on her at Christmas to make sure she wasn't alone."

"That was so kind of you."

"The only time Eleanor really paid attention was when Marci got into trouble or got hurt doing something foolhardy." She chuckled. "I'm not sure she's grown out of that either, judging from the cane she was leaning on when I ran into her recently at the college."

Despite the insight into how she'd reacted as a child, Bridgette couldn't let go of her exasperation with Ryder's life-risking behavior as an adult. "Some people never outgrow their childhood." She flushed at the judgment in her voice and squirmed under Trudy's thoughtful gaze.

"Still, she's grown into a beautiful young woman." Trudy said. "Eleanor would have been proud."

"Yes. I'm sure you're right." She didn't want to have this discussion with Trudy or anybody else.

Trudy seemed to understand and stood. "Well, dear, I've taken enough of your time. I had only stopped by to ask for an invitation to the auction. I'd like to see if there's a piece my old friend painted that strikes my fancy."

"Of course. The invitations went out to collectors and art agents several weeks ago. I'm sorry that we've overlooked her friends here."

"No worries. There aren't many of us. Eleanor mostly kept to herself."

Bridgette grabbed a handful of invitations from the stack of paperwork on the table and handed them to her. "Please, give one of these to anyone else who would like to come."

"Thank you, dear." Trudy patted her hand. "Marci's so lucky to have such good friends. She'll realize one day that she's not as alone as she thinks."

Chapter Nineteen

"S he fainted? Skyler fainted?"

Tory laughed. "She is human, you know."

Ryder and Tory stood outside the nursery, scanning the rows of bassinets for the one marked Parker-Reese. It had been a long, tense night, with the baby finally arriving around six that morning.

"They weren't expecting to do a C-section," Tory said. "Dr. Nichols said Sky hit the floor like a load of bricks when they cut Jess open. They managed to get her on her feet to see the baby before they took Jess to recovery, but Skyler was too shaky to hold her."

"Hey, there she is now."

A door opened opposite from the windows where they stood, and a nurse led Skyler to a bassinet on the back row and showed her how to properly hold little Leigh Parker-Reese—named after Jessica's grandmother, the Parker matriarch. The nurse pointed to a rocking chair in the corner and Skyler took a seat, her gaze on the small figure swaddled in her arms.

They saw her wipe away a tear and grin when the nurse said something to her.

"Is she crying? I can't believe she's crying."

"I can't imagine what she must be feeling," Tory said softly.

"She's different," Ryder said, struggling to put words to her tangled emotions.

"I hope so." Tory slid her arm over Ryder's shoulders. "When you fall in love, it changes you. It changes everything."

"Not gonna happen to me," she said, frowning at Skyler brushing the tip of her finger along the baby's cheek. "I can't see me doing that."

"You don't know what you're capable of until you meet the right person."

She should feel happy for her friends. Instead, she felt like she was watching them board a train going someplace new and she didn't have a ticket. Was Tory going, too?

"So, you gonna knock Leah up?"

Tory laughed again and grabbed her by the back of the neck to shake her. "Don't you dare say 'knocked up' in front of Leah."

Tory released her and they watched Skyler rock the baby.

"Leah and I haven't talked about it. I grew up with two brothers and kind of enjoy the peace and quiet of just the two of us. But if she decides she wants to have children, I'm okay with that."

"Not me. I'm not relationship material. I can't even keep a house plant alive."

Tory looked at her. "I thought you and Bridgette might have something going."

"No. We don't." Her throat worked around the words that choked her. "And I have to get back to Dallas. My agent e-mailed. If I can get the rodeo to clear me to compete, I still have time to qualify for the nationals."

"I thought you'd be here another month or so."

"I'm already packed and flying out tonight. In fact, I need to leave if I'm going to catch a plane out of Richmond in four hours."

Tory scowled. "Were you even going to say good-bye?"

She shrugged. "I'm not really good with that. Tell Sky and Jess thanks for everything. I'll e-mail them when I get back to Dallas."

Tory stared at her, then pulled her into a tight hug. "You've got family here, little sister, whether you think so or not," Tory whispered in her ear. "And if you don't show up here for Christmas, Skyler and I are flying out and hauling your ass back here. You understand? Don't leave and stay gone for so long again."

"Yeah, I hear you."

She did understand, but she wasn't leaving them. They'd already left her. Her friends had grown up and settled down. They'd changed and she hadn't. She was still and always would be the one left behind.

❖

The glass of wine before her sat untouched as Bridgette settled onto a large square pillow and relaxed into a lotus position. She concentrated on the trickle of the stream below the balcony where she worked to empty her thoughts.

Her focus gradually switched from the sounds of the water to the thump of her own heartbeat, and it slowed to the point she could almost hear the squish of her blood flowing in and out with every contraction of the thick muscle. Her mind became a blank, black slate as she mentally floated.

Then the beat of her heart developed an odd, faint echo. It didn't feel threatening. It felt comforting, as though she wasn't alone in her void. Curious, she reached deeper—deep enough to touch the place she had walled off long ago. The terror that usually met her there was absent, and she cautiously opened the mental door.

Stephan poured out.

This time, she didn't have memories of blood and bulls but happy memories of childhood, running and laughing together. He beckoned and she followed. A hot wind lifted her hair and danced among the strands like a caress. He lifted his hands to the sky and she saw the storm clouds, dark and turbulent, roiling with sheet lightning.

She stared up at the storm and realized it was familiar. The abstract. She was looking at the painting in the small upstairs studio. This wasn't her storm, so she didn't have any reason to shrink from it. Still, it did frighten her, just in a different way.

She could hear the old monk's voice. *Control your fear and it can keep you safe. Unleash your fear and, like a fierce tiger, it will hunt and cripple you.*

Before she could consider this, a *tap-tap* at her consciousness drew her from her meditation. As she surfaced, she realized the tapping came from raindrops, cold and wet, falling on her face and arms. The Indian-summer shower gained momentum and she lifted her face to let the downpour wash over her.

Her laughter bubbled up. She had let herself feel Stephan and she didn't hurt. She felt lighter, almost weightless. She had stood in the dark storm that was Ryder's torment and found her own had calmed. She grabbed her wineglass and pillow to dash back into the loft.

She didn't hesitate, fitting the crowbar under the wood and prying the crate open. She lifted them out, one by one, until all six paintings were propped against the wall. They were her storm—bitter, tormented evidence of her grief.

She sank to the floor, tears mingling now with the raindrops that lingered on her skin. This time, they weren't tears of loss but tears of relief. The pain that tore at her was gone. She realized at last that Stephan's death was not about hurting her. He had jumped in front of those charging bulls for his own reasons. Reasons she would never understand, but then they weren't hers to own.

She did know Ryder's reasons. The paintings in that child's studio were as clear as a storybook. If only she could get Ryder to see that she must face her tiger, too.

What I don't understand is why it matters to you.

She wasn't ready to answer Ryder's question, not even for herself. But she did need to see Ryder. One tiger at a time.

❖

"Come on in." Skyler waved for Bridgette to follow her. "Jess just finished feeding the baby. We're hanging out in the den."

"I don't mean to intrude. I was looking for Marc. Is she here?"

"Ryder? She skipped out on us a few days ago. I'm going to kick her butt when I see her again for not saying a proper good-bye."

"She's returned to Dallas?"

"Yeah. She told Tory that her agent e-mailed. Apparently he's anxious to get her back to work before the buzz dies down over the article Leah wrote."

Bridgette stopped. "And you let her go? She just suffered a concussion."

Skyler narrowed her eyes. "Nobody *lets* Ryder do anything. She does what she wants. Always has." She started down the hall again. "Come say hey to Jess and your future art student."

Jessica was propped up on the sofa and lifted her feet when Skyler returned so she could slide in under her legs to sit close enough to touch the baby sleeping in her arms.

"Jess, she's precious. What a head of hair!"

Jessica smiled up at her. "She's got Skyler's thick, blond hair."

"And Jess's blue eyes," Skyler said.

"Honey, you know that can change in the next few weeks."

"Nope. Leigh and I talked about this. She agrees that her eyes should stay blue."

Jessica shook her head. "I'm sorry, we're kind of sappy about the whole baby thing."

Bridgette laughed and sat in the chair adjacent to Jessica, distracted from thinking about Ryder for the moment. "I'd be worried if you weren't."

"I'm sure we'll be ready to shove her off on our friends to babysit by the time she hits the terrible twos," Skyler said.

"I'm sure."

"Do you want to hold her?"

"I do, but I don't want to wake her. I just stopped by for a minute." She sat back, then forward again to extract the rattle toy that was poking her in the back. "I came to see Marc, but Skyler said she's gone back to Dallas."

Skyler and Jessica shared a look she couldn't decipher. What had Ryder told them about their—she wasn't sure herself what to call it— encounters? Did they blame her for Ryder's abrupt departure? She really didn't feel like explaining what had happened between them. She wasn't sure she could.

"We found some additional artwork in her grandmother's house, and I need to speak with her about it. I'm sure she'll want to keep it." It wasn't really a lie. "But I guess I'm too late."

Jessica seemed to consider her words before she shifted the baby into Skyler's arms and swung her feet to the floor. "I have her contact information in the office. I'll get it for you."

"Don't go to any trouble. I'm sure her lawyer can get in touch with her."

"It's no trouble," Jessica said as she stood. "I need a bathroom break anyway."

Skyler smiled down at the baby, who had opened her eyes and was curling her small hand around Skyler's finger. "Hey, you. Do you want to meet your Aunt Bridgette?" She looked up. "Come sit over here if you want to hold her. If you don't, that's okay. Not everybody's into babies."

"I'd love to." She moved to the sofa and Skyler gently placed the baby in her arms. "Hello, little Leigh," she cooed. "I'm your Aunt

Bridgette and, when you're old enough, I'm going to teach you how to finger-paint and draw and make the prettiest pictures for your moms."

Unable to keep her hands away, Skyler offered her finger again and Leigh immediately wrapped her tiny hand around it.

"I would have never imagined this—having a family of my own and being who I am today," Skyler said, more to herself than anyone listening. "I guess finding Jess helped me believe I could be something more, something better." Skyler looked at her. "Some of the kids in the Young Equestrian Program have really troubled home situations, so I'm taking some online classes in child psychology. I'd have never thought about doing that before."

"That's wonderful, Sky." She wondered if Ryder could ever see her future differently.

"Here you go."

She handed the baby back to Skyler and stood to take the paper Jessica offered. "Thanks. I hate to run, but I've got to prepare an exam for my art-history class."

"I'll walk you out," Jessica said, trailing after her.

She paused in the sunlight that dappled the wide porch. "Will I see you two at the auction?"

"You'll probably see three of us. The grandmas are here, upstairs napping. They still haven't adjusted to our time zone. I'm sure Kate and Mom will want to check out the auction. I have a feeling Skyler will insist on staying home with the baby, so I'll probably come with them. I may want to bid on something."

"Good. I'll look forward to meeting them."

She could tell Jessica wanted to say more, so she waited.

"There's a lot more to Ryder than she lets most people see," Jessica said softly. "I wasn't sure I'd like the cocky flirt that showed up here six weeks ago. But we became pretty good friends while she was here, and I realized that under all that bravado is a real sweetheart."

"Jess—" Her heart already knew this, but the bravado that made Ryder take stupid risks was a hurdle Bridgette still couldn't get past. It was a shield she wasn't sure Ryder could let go.

"Whatever's between you two is none of my business, but if you talk to her, tell her I miss my workout buddy."

Bridgette nodded. She missed Ryder, too. Fiercely. "I will."

CHAPTER TWENTY

R yder left all thoughts of Bridgette and Cherokee Falls at her Dallas condo when she drove to the rodeo arena. She couldn't have anything but the beast and the ride on her mind for the next eight-or-so hours.

The men were provided a locker room where they traded jokes and information about the rides they had drawn as they prepared for their event. She wasn't exactly welcomed there, and after a few such facilities offered only open showers and dressing areas, she took advantage of her inherited wealth and had an RV customized for her own personal dressing room that she could drive and park at any rodeo event.

Even with the RV, she was glad the Texas Stampede was the last big event before the nationals. Held on the outskirts of Dallas, it meant she could park her dressing room at the arena grounds and still drive her car home to sleep in her own bed each night.

Being at her best was critical this week. Only the Professional Rodeo Cowboys Association's top fifteen money-winners for the year would be invited to the National Finals Rodeo in Vegas, and the other competitors had been racking up winnings while she was recuperating. She'd had a spectacular year leading up to her injury, but she would need to place well this week to stay in the top fifteen.

Bareback bronc riding today, bull riding on Saturday. She competed in only the two events.

The hours-long ritual to transform into a rodeo gladiator began with a long hot shower and thorough shave, arms and legs. Next came fifteen minutes of stretching while she mentally evaluated every muscle in her legs, groin, arms, shoulders, and back. She felt good.

By the tail end of the rodeo season, the riders were all sore and beat-up from weekend after weekend of grueling competition. But Ryder's few months off had given her shoulder and back muscles time to recuperate, while her gym workouts had maintained her strength.

She tugged on thigh-length compression shorts but no bra, because she wrapped her torso in a wide Ace bandage from waist to armpit to support her back muscles.

She used to pay a sports trainer to tape her, but once she learned the process, she preferred solitude as she also mentally prepared for the ride. She began with her knees, applying liquid adhesive, winding the thin pre-wrap from shin to thigh, then topping it with strong, white adhesive tape.

She taped her right wrist and hand that would grip the rigging, then taped custom-molded plastic guards to her left shin and her left forearm, where metal plates were screwed into the bones. A tight, long-sleeved compression shirt went on top to support the tendons and ligaments of her shoulders.

Then she dressed. Wrangler jeans, a colorful Western shirt adorned with the logos of her sponsors, worn Tony Lama boots, and wide bat-wing chaps. The clothing covered all clues of her first ninety minutes of preparation. Only the tape on her hand peeked out of her sleeve, and a thick glove would cover that before she broke from the gate.

After another fifteen minutes of stretching, she dropped her bareback rigging onto the floor and plopped down to straddle the handle. For the next twenty minutes, she repeatedly stretched her legs forward and pulled them back—heels to ass—as she rode the horse in her head.

She was ready. Now came the hated waiting.

She paused briefly to sign a few autographs, but talked little as she headed across the parking lot to the arena. Her mind was on the ride.

She walked the long tunnel that wrapped around the lower level of the indoor facility, crowded now with competitors, judges, roadies, and equipment that were the trappings of the event. The announcer's voice was piped into the tunnel, keeping everyone advised of how the schedule was progressing. She was happy to hear that barrel racing was already wrapping up.

The first broncs were being led into the staging area. These were not wild animals. Most were as docile as puppies until a rider dropped onto their back and the bucking strap pulled snug around their bellies.

Ryder coughed the arena dust from her lungs and dropped her equipment bag to complete the last of her ritual. She was fourth up for her first of three rides, so she wouldn't have to wait long. Still, she always saved a few tasks to occupy her in the dead time before she could climb into the chute.

She strapped on her lucky spurs, carefully dulled and free-spinning to meet regulations that prevented harm to the animal's hide. Next, she wound a long leather thong tight under the arch and around the outside of each boot shaft several times and tied it off to prevent the boots from slipping off as she spurred during the ride.

She was pleased she had drawn Red River Skoal, a top gelding who would certainly be selected for the nationals. He was alert today, ears flicking forward and back as she talked to him in a low voice. She liked to rig her ride herself and chuckled as Skoal shook his entire body like a wet dog when she cinched up the latigo straps of soft cotton girth. He was feeling good, and that meant a good buck and a top score.

While a roadie led the horse to the chute, she slipped on a protective vest with a stiff foam roll in the collar to protect her neck from whiplash and settled her Stetson low over her brow. She'd probably lose it during the ride, but a real cowboy never broke the gate hatless.

The crowd roared, but she didn't look up as she climbed over the railing of the chute and carefully lowered herself onto the horse's back. She didn't care how the guy before her was doing or if the leaderboard had changed. She didn't have anything in her mind now but Red River Skoal and the ride.

"Too bad for Kip Brown. Black Betty is a tough one," the announcer said cheerfully. "Hopefully, he'll have better luck on his next ride."

Ryder tested the tie on the heavy leather glove encasing her right hand and then pulled her gloved fingers through the snug handle of the rigging. Skoal shifted restlessly under her.

"Next up, we welcome Marc Ryder. Our only female competitor in bronc and bull riding, this will be Ms. Ryder's first event since a bad meeting with a bull put her out of competition for a few months. She's drawn a good ride for the occasion, Red River Skoal, two-time national bucking horse of the year."

She leaned back and straightened her legs to lift her spurs above the horse's shoulders. Riders were disqualified if they failed to "mark out" their ride, meaning they had to keep their spurs in that position until the bronc's front feet touched the ground after breaking from the gate.

She stared down at her mount and uttered the good-luck charm that completed her ritual. "Flyin' ain't hard. You just throw yourself at the ground and miss."

She popped in her mouthpiece and raised her left hand high over her head. She gave a firm nod and the chute steward yanked the bucking strap tight at the same time the gate swung open.

Legs forward as Skoal's heels went skyward, then spurs to ass as the horse reared. Rear, kick, turn, rear and launch upward, then down hard with heels nearly vertical to the ground. Crow hop on all fours, then back to the rear, buck, rear, buck.

It was a textbook ride.

While bull riding is the most dangerous, bareback bronc riding is considered the most physical of the rodeo events. The faster, more energetic buck of the horse flings the rider back and forth like a rag doll. But few horses buck with the body twist favored by the bulls, and Ryder found their rolling motion much easier to follow.

At the sound of the buzzer, she abandoned her usual gymnastic-style dismount that won her points with the crowd and waited for the pickup men to sandwich her bronc between their horses so she could slide up behind one of them and be deposited gently on solid ground.

She didn't need the crowd's roar to know she had done well. She had felt the perfect rhythm of it. Hell, her hat was even still sitting securely on her head. But she pulled it off now and waved it at the cheering fans when the scoreboard flashed a high eighty-eight for her ride.

That score was her best, but her other two rides went pretty much the same. At the end of the day, she placed a close second to the winner. So she wasn't surprised when Ashley waved her over to the ESPN camera for an interview.

Blond and lithe, Ashley was a former barrel-racing champ who had hung up her chaps when she married and started having babies. She was just Ryder's type, and they'd hooked up once. But Ashley was more straight than bisexual, and they both wrote it off as a good time.

Ryder's hair had grown long enough that it was starting to curl around her collar, and Ashley eyed it critically. "Not a bad look. It could use some styling, but I like it longer," she said.

Ryder lifted her hat to brush her hair back from her face. "Don't get used to it. I'm getting it cut tomorrow."

Ashley shrugged. "Ready?"

"Yeah. Let's do it."

They turned and waited for the cameraman's cue.

"That was a spectacular return after several months off the circuit. How'd it feel out there today?"

"It felt good. Real good. I think the layoff actually helped. Everybody else is sore and tired from the long rodeo season, but I'm rested and ready to go."

"How ready will you be for the bulls on Saturday? You suffered some pretty bad injuries the last time you rode one. No reservations about getting back out there?"

Actually, it was a cold ball of fear in her belly that she actively nurtured. It helped block out the ache that squeezed her chest so tight she couldn't breathe every time she thought of Bridgette. But fear wasn't what her fans paid to see.

She tipped her hat back and grinned at the camera.

Bridgette smiled and waved at the two students sitting in the grass when one held up her art-history book in a gesture that said "We're studying for your exam," even though they'd been studying each other's tonsils—not their art history—a moment before they spotted her.

She loved this college campus. Her heart bloomed with its abundant trees and flowers every spring. She relaxed with the shorts and flip-flop atmosphere of the summer term, and the artist in her thrilled at the explosion of color that each fall brought to the foothills where Cherokee Falls was nestled. She felt lighter, unfettered, walking now among the peak of this year's spectacular autumn palette.

There was still the matter of Marc. She didn't want to abandon her like others had done. She *had* survived opening the dreaded crate, but Marc was a new risk. She flushed at the thought of her. Maybe a bigger risk than Stephan.

Marc was passion and tenderness and mind-numbing hot sex. A cliff with an edge waiting to crumble under her feet. A parachute that might not open.

She would think about that later. She had Marc's contact information. Maybe she'd e-mail her. Maybe she'd wait to see if she would show up at Skyler and Jessica's for Christmas. It was a little less than two months away, but time she needed to examine her feelings.

She pushed through the doors of the student center on her mission to secure a large chai latte, an essential part of her exam-writing routine. The questions were already taking shape in her head.

But as she circled around the lounge area, a familiar husky voice stopped her. Twenty or more students were gathered before the big-screen television where a larger-than-life Marc Ryder peeled her eyes off the pretty blond ESPN sportscaster, tilted her Stetson back, and grinned at the camera.

"I love riding bulls. If it wasn't dangerous, it wouldn't be as much fun. Saturday can't get here fast enough for me."

"Besides the thrill, what makes the bulls special?"

"The challenge. They aren't as neat and predictable as broncs. They twist and spin and throw their horns back. When you're up on that bull, you don't have room to think about anything but staying on his back and away from those horns."

"A lot of riders who suffered the injuries you did would consider retiring from bull riding. What drives you to get back out there?"

Ryder shrugged. "It's not really anything driving me, just nothing stopping me."

"Well, there was certainly nothing stopping you today. Congratulations for your success and good luck on Saturday." The blonde turned to the camera as it moved in for a close-up. "Marc

Ryder, still making a name for herself in an almost exclusively male sport, celebrating an excellent return to the rodeo circuit today and looking forward to Saturday's bull riding. Back to you, Jim."

The picture switched to three cowboys in a studio.

"Bull riding is certainly a dangerous sport and not for the faint of heart," Jim told the camera before turning to his co-announcers. "And a lot of people think it's no place for a woman. What do you think, Ty?"

"I think an athlete is an athlete," the middle-aged cowboy in the Western-print shirt said. "There are sports where women aren't physically big enough to compete against men, like basketball and football. But rodeo requires only strength and timing. If a woman is strong enough and skilled enough, then I say go for it."

"What about you, Jimmy? There certainly weren't any women competing with the men when you were rodeoing."

The old cowboy wearing a stylish white Resistol winked at the camera. "Well, Jim, my daddy used to say you gotta be a little stupid and a lot tough to ride bulls. I've known some pretty tough women in my day. If one of them is stupid enough to climb up on two thousand pounds of meanness, then I wouldn't stand in her way."

"Two thousand pounds of meanness is exactly what Marc Ryder encountered her last time out."

The picture cut away to a video clip of Ryder settling onto the back of a huge black bull. Then the gate swung open and the bull launched into the arena, spinning and bucking.

Bridgette unconsciously rubbed her arm as she watched Ryder being jerked this way and that as the bull constantly changed directions. When the eight-second buzzer sounded, she tensed.

Instead of lying back on the bull, Ryder was hunched forward, working her hand loose from the rigging, when the bull kicked his heels high again. She pitched forward at the same time the bull threw his head back, and her forehead banged against the unyielding base of the bull's horns.

The students groaned. "That's gotta hurt," one boy remarked.

Tears stung Bridgette's eyes as though the blow had been to her own forehead. Don't look, don't look. But she was paralyzed, unable to turn away as Ryder's limp body slid off the bull onto the ground.

The rodeo clowns leapt into action, but Ryder's body jerked several times as the bull's heels came down on her leg, bounced up, and came down again before a clown could get the animal's attention.

He snorted and pawed at the ground, preparing to charge. The clowns waved bandanas and shouted. One clown taunted from behind a large padded barrel, daring the bull to charge to the other side of the arena. For a minute, it appeared that he would. Two roadies edged over the top of the railing, ready to jump into the arena and drag Ryder to safety.

Then the bull wheeled and, instead, charged the figure sprawled and unmoving. He plowed his horns into the dirt to root under Ryder and throw her into the air. She hit facedown and he snagged one curved horn under the back of her vest.

The bull stomped again on her injured leg, then lifted and shook his great head as Ryder dangled from his horn. He tossed her into the air a second time. One fearless clown rushed forward to grab the bull's tail and give it hard crank. When the bull whirled, the clown was halfway to the barrel. The animal gave chase and the clown jumped into the barrel a split second before the bull rammed into it.

The heavy barrel rolled away and the bull stood, snorting. He swung his body back toward Ryder, but two men were already there, each slipping a hand in the armholes of her vest to grab hold. Ryder raised her hand, then dropped it again as they dragged her away.

The students cheered. "Show it again, show it again," they chanted.

Bridgette sprinted to the restroom and vomited her lunch in the first empty stall. A couple of students looked at her curiously when she emerged, and she quickly rinsed her mouth at the sink.

Marc's fine. She's fine. She was walking around Cherokee Falls just last week. She's not dead, not paralyzed, not crippled. She's fine.

But the mantra in Bridgette's head didn't stop the second wave of nausea, and she hurried to the art building next door, slamming into her office and falling to her knees in the small bathroom. Her gagging soon turned to weak sobs.

Marc. Baby.

The thought of her being tossed about like a doll wasn't what crushed her now. It was thinking of Marc, in pain, alone in the hospital. Was there anyone who held her hand, wiped her brow, and spooned ice chips into her mouth after surgery?

It was too late to push her away, too late to be friends. At that moment, she knew with concrete certainty that she was in love with Marc Ryder.

Losing Stephan hurt because she had wanted him to always be there for her.

This was different. She wanted to be the one who was there for Marc, holding her, loving her, healing hurts and protecting her from new ones.

Even worse, she knew Marc was in love with her. She had known it, had felt it the night they made love in Eleanor's mansion.

She covered her face with her hands and groaned. What was she going to do?

"It's not really anything driving me, just nothing stopping me."

She climbed to her feet and hunched over the sink to splash her burning eyes with cold water. She dried her face and straightened.

She needed to see Marc. She stuffed her exam materials into her laptop bag.

The two of them had to stop running—from their fears and from each other. It was time to pony up, and she wasn't taking this ride alone.

CHAPTER TWENTY-ONE

It was three in the morning, and Marc looked adorable.

She had answered the door in black boy shorts and a faded T-shirt with the logo of a jumping horse and slogan that said GRAND NATIONAL HUNT AT AINTREE. She had cut her dark hair short, and the spikes stood up like a halo. Her eyes were sleepy, her mouth open in surprise. She blinked.

"God, I hope this isn't just a dream."

"No talking," Bridgette said. She pushed Marc back into the condo and followed her inside. She closed the door and locked it. "You just need to listen."

"Bridge—"

She pinned Marc against the wall.

"I said no talking."

She brought her mouth close, as close to Marc's as possible without touching. She ran her hands under Marc's shirt and smiled when she jerked. Her hands wouldn't be cold for long because Marc's skin was warm and soft as velvet. Her nipples were hard.

"Pay close attention to everything I'm saying to you," she whispered.

And then she kissed her. She kissed Marc tenderly with every emotion she'd been holding back, then deeper with every ounce of passion that bloomed inside her. She kissed her until she moaned, they both moaned, and Marc sagged against the wall.

"Where's your bedroom?"

Marc started to answer, then closed her mouth and pointed. She took Marc's hand and led her upstairs to stand beside the king-sized bed where, moments before, Marc had been sleeping. She hadn't considered the possibility, but she paused to mentally thank the gods another woman wasn't snuggled among those rumpled covers.

"Watch, but don't touch," she said softly as she stepped back and began to undress.

She slid her blouse from her shoulders and Marc stared at her breasts. She swirled her middle fingers over her own erect nipples, their outline clear under the silky material of her bra. Marc licked her lips in anticipation and her gaze locked on Bridgette's chest as she slowly reached behind to unclasp her bra and let it drop to the floor. She pinched her own nipples and groaned. Marc's hands twitched.

Then she turned her back to Marc and slowly lowered her jeans and panties in one movement. She heard Marc suck in a breath when she bent over to slip off her shoes and remove the clothes now pooled around her ankles. Marc's hands were moving again as she faced her.

"No touching until I say so."

Marc's hands twisted the tail of her T-shirt in an effort to restrain them. Her eyes were no longer soft and dazed. They were hungry.

She went to Marc and caressed her cheek, then freed her hands from their entanglement. "Off," she said, tugging the shirt upward until Marc raised her arms to let her remove it.

Bridgette edged closer until their nipples were almost touching. Almost.

"You are a warrior goddess," she murmured, running her fingertips down Marc's sides and blowing gently across the stiff nipples. Her mouth watered to suck them, but she would get to that later. "I don't think I've ever seen a stronger, more beautiful female body."

She drifted slowly lower, until she was on her knees, and drew the boy shorts down Marc's hard thighs. She breathed in the scent of Marc's arousal and, without stopping to think, buried her nose in the dark, wet curls. Marc trembled under her hands and she knew this was how she'd claim her first.

She gently pushed Marc down onto the bed and shouldered her legs. Propped on her elbows, Marc watched her, eyes blazing as

Bridgette rubbed her cheek against her thigh and met her gaze. Could Marc see how much she wanted her?

"I love the way you smell." She smoothed her hands up Marc's taut belly and brushed her palms over her breasts. "I love the way you feel. Hard, yet so soft." She fingered Marc's rigid nipples, rolling them between her thumb and fingers until Marc closed her eyes and moaned.

Then she tasted her, salty and sweet. Marc's clit was firm under her tongue, and she wasted no time sucking it into her mouth and scraping her teeth across the swollen flesh.

"Bridgette. Oh, Christ. I can't—"

She filled Marc with two fingers, stroking her inside and out. Marc's breath hitched and her body bucked. But she held on, riding out Marc's orgasm until she collapsed, panting and jerking with the aftershocks.

She wiped her wet cheeks against Marc's belly, but kept her fingers inside as she moved to lie beside her. She kissed Marc's slack mouth, laving her tongue across the full lips before plunging inside. When Marc responded, dancing their tongues together, she began to stroke with her fingers again. Marc whimpered but opened her legs, surrendering to her.

She moved over Marc to straddle her thigh and assuage her own burning need as she added a third finger. She thrust, slowly and gently at first, and Marc slid her hand down to wedge her fingers between her thigh and Bridgette's sex to reciprocate. She pumped harder and with purpose, and Marc moved with her.

Marc's eyes widened when she pressed her pinkie lower, against her small puckered ring of muscle, but she didn't protest as Bridgette plunged the small digit inside. She laid her thumb against Marc's clit and held her gaze as she took her completely.

Something fragile and fleeting flashed in Marc's eyes. Usually quiet and restrained in her orgasms, she dropped her head back and roared with her climax, soaking Bridgette's hand. Marc's fingers convulsed against her sex, triggering her orgasm, too.

They were both slick with exertion and desire when she collapsed, spent yet unsated. She didn't worry whether the strong body under hers could bear her physical weight. But could the heart that beat against hers hold up under what she was feeling, what she was still afraid to confess?

She felt Marc's chest hitch and caught a glimpse of tears before she turned her face away. She bit back the words that had been on the tip of her tongue, and they lodged in her throat to choke her.

She gently withdrew her hand and dried it on the cast-off T-shirt. Marc took a deep breath and rolled them to the other side of the king-sized bed, holding Bridgette tight against her.

"Stay." Marc's voice was low and rough, almost pleading.

She snuggled against Marc's neck and gentled her with her hands. She felt Marc slowly relax, and she did, too. The late hour, the long day, and the emotion of their coupling had exhausted them. Her deep sigh matched Marc's as they found comfort in the intimate warmth of skin on skin and let sleep claim them.

They would have time for words later.

Ryder woke with Bridgette spooned in the curve of her body, warm in her arms. When Bridgette shifted onto her back, the sheet pooled around her waist and Ryder studied her in the early morning light.

She was beautiful.

She fingered the blond curls that spread across the pillow. Her gaze caressed the fine planes of her brow, sculpted bones of her cheeks, and the soft, full lashes that fluttered as Bridgette dreamed. She itched to kiss Bridgette's soft breasts. When she looked up again, drowsy hazel eyes were watching her.

"Hi," she said softly.

"Good morning." Bridgette covered her mouth with her hand. "I probably have morning breath."

She pulled her hand away. "Let me see." She kissed her, gently pushing her tongue into Bridgette's mouth and tasting her. "Mmm." She pulled back. "No morning breath, but you do smell like sex…in a good way."

She had slept only a few hours, but it was the deepest, most restorative rest she could remember experiencing. She hadn't realized how much energy she exerted each day to keep up the wall that guarded her feelings. She'd been building that wall since she was a child, but Bridgette had come to her and obliterated it the night before, if only briefly. Her heart jerked. What now?

"Just happen to be in the neighborhood?" Her voice sounded more casual than she felt.

Uncertainty flashed in Bridgette's eyes and she pulled the sheet up to cover her chest. "I flew out here to talk with you."

"About the auction?"

Bridgette's hand trembled and she covered it with hers, entwining their fingers.

"About us." Bridgette took a deep breath, avoiding her eyes. "But now that I'm here, I'm not sure where to start."

Words were never easy for her, either. They had only spoken their feelings with their bodies, and she was suddenly terrified they would fail in a conversation with words.

"Come shower with me and I'll make some breakfast. Then we'll talk."

Bridgette seemed relieved at the reprieve and allowed her to draw the sheet down and feather kisses across her shoulders and breasts. She took Bridgette's hand to lead her into the large, decadent bathroom. Bridgette smiled as she surveyed the Italian tile, triple-head shower, and the whirlpool half sunk into the floor under a large one-way window.

"What can I say? I'm a hedonist."

She released Bridgette so they could brush their teeth while the water warmed, and then they stepped in together. She carefully washed Bridgette's hair for her, and then they teasingly soaped each other's bodies.

The night before, she had given control to Bridgette, something she had never done with another woman. But Bridgette seemed tentative this morning, and she was determined to reinforce what they'd shared.

Drawing Bridgette to her under the heated spray, she kissed her deeply. Their hips, their breasts fit perfectly together. She pressed her against the warmed tile and slowly kissed her way down. When she finally knelt before her, she carefully guided Bridgette's legs onto her broad shoulders, opening her as she balanced against the shower's wall.

She gazed up at Bridgette for a long moment before she pressed her face into her sex, bathing her with broad strokes of her tongue until Bridgette squirmed.

"Marc, oh, God, Marc."

She burned the words into her memory. No one had ever, would ever utter her name with such passion. No one had ever, would ever touch her so deep. She wanted to cry and sing at the same time.

"Please, darling. Make me come." Bridgette's voice trembled with her need.

As much as she wanted it to last forever, she was helpless against Bridgette's plea. She flicked her tongue over the hard tissue, then sucked her until Bridgette climaxed. She stroked her through her orgasm with the flat of her tongue, then quickly stood and wrapped Bridgette's legs around her hips. She pumped her swollen clit against Bridgette's heat quickly and growled out her own orgasm.

She let Bridgette regain her feet but kept her pressed against the wall, her forehead resting on Bridgette's shoulder.

"Do you know how beautiful you are?" she murmured. Did Bridgette know she was in love with her?

Bridgette sighed and stroked her back. "I need coffee, and then we need to talk, Marc."

She nodded but didn't speak.

They dried each other wordlessly, then dressed and went downstairs to the kitchen where she brewed coffee, warmed bagels, and quickly scrambled eggs for them. They sat at the table for two and picked at the food for a while before Bridgette finally found the words to begin.

"You scare me," she said.

She was surprised and a little irritated at that confession. "Scare you? I scare *you*? Every time we get close, you disappear on me. I feel tossed back and forth, worse than the first time I rode a bronc. Is sex all you want from me?" She was so bad at this. She wanted to say something different, something sweet. Instead, she sounded like a petulant child.

"No." Bridgette stared down at her plate. "But what I want, what I need might be more than you can give."

She put down her fork and took Bridgette's hand. "Ask me. We can't know unless you ask."

"Quit this insane rodeo thing and come back to Cherokee Falls with me."

She released Bridgette's hand and sat back. A million things churned through her thoughts. Was Bridgette asking for a relationship? Her request hadn't included any promise in return. Was she just a concerned fuck-buddy?

The rodeo was a cruel lover. But, unlike the people who had deserted or ignored her without explanation, the rules of that relationship were clear. The spotlight, the fans were hers as long as she performed. It didn't seem to work that way with people.

"What would you say if I asked you to give up being an artist?"

"It's not the same thing."

"Isn't it?"

"I'm not risking my life when I paint."

"What if I was a police officer or a firefighter?"

"You're not. And that's not the same as needlessly risking your life." Bridgette put her hand up to forestall her argument. "Just listen, okay?"

She nodded, then waited silently as Bridgette sipped her coffee.

"When I was growing up, we moved a lot—all over the world—because of my father's career. I always made friends wherever we lived, but it's impossible to form close, lasting friendships when you only stay in one place, one country for a few years at a time. So my best friend was my older brother, Stephan."

She took another sip.

"My parents were great, but Stephan was my champion and my confidant. I depended on him. He stood beside me when I told my parents I was gay, and he was there for me when my first girlfriend dumped me. I also could count on him to be my most honest art critic."

She looked up to meet Ryder's gaze.

"And he was reckless with his life. He knew how important he was to me, but that didn't matter when he needed an adrenaline fix. He climbed mountains, jumped from airplanes, and even scuba-dived among sharks once. He seemed…he thought he was invincible. But he wasn't."

Tears filled Bridgette's eyes.

"We had rented a villa on the coast of Spain for our annual vacation together, but he wanted to go to Pamplona for the running of the bulls. He said he wanted to watch from the street level, but I stayed in our hotel room on the balcony. When they came running down the street, a bull gored a man through the chest right below me."

She choked back a sob, and Ryder rounded the table to gather Bridgette in her arms. "Shhh. You don't have to tell me."

But Bridgette shook her head and continued.

"It was awful. There was so much blood. Some men ran into the street to pull him behind a barrier, and when they turned him over, it was Stephan. I had no idea he could be that foolish. He died that night in a Spanish hospital."

Ryder held her tight, wishing she could take her pain from her. But Bridgette pulled back.

"I felt betrayed that I wasn't important enough for him to be careful with his life. He knew how much I needed him, but he left me anyway."

She took Bridgette's hands in hers. "Listen to me carefully. There is a huge difference between what your brother did and what I'm going to do tomorrow."

Bridgette tried to tug her hands free, but she held tight.

"Stay and you'll see. I'll spend half a day suiting up with protective gear before I ever climb into that chute. I'm not some inexperienced amateur wearing nothing but loose clothing and a red sash."

Bridgette shook her head. "It has taken me years to come to terms with Stephan's death. I can't bear that kind of loss again. It would destroy me."

Could she do what Bridgette was asking?

"It's not as simple as deciding not to ride tomorrow. My sponsors, my agent, the rodeo are depending on me. ESPN has been hyping my return to the circuit so much that half the audience will be tuned in just to see me ride that bull or get dumped on my ass. I can't back out now."

Bridgette yanked her hands away and crossed her arms over her chest. "Those are just excuses, Marc. You could withdraw if you really wanted. This is about you, not other people. You need to be honest with yourself about why you really need to do this."

She paced across the room and back. Bridgette wasn't even trying to understand. Couldn't she see this was different? That she wasn't Stephan? She didn't need to be psychoanalyzed. She just needed to ride that bull. Her anger rose before she could temper her bitter words.

"You want to know what real pain is, Bridgette? The people who left me didn't die. They left because they just didn't care."

But Bridgette wasn't swayed. She raised her voice to match Ryder's. "You know what? Here's the real problem. Despite my best efforts to stay away, I've fallen in love with you, damn it." She walked quickly to the door and picked up her purse where she'd dropped it the night before. "But I can't live in constant fear that I'll lose you. If you really need to ride that bull tomorrow, we're done."

CHAPTER TWENTY-TWO

Stunned, Ryder stood frozen. The slamming of the front door echoed in her ears.

I've fallen in love with you.

She turned the statement over in her mind. Nobody had ever said that to her. Nobody. Ever.

Oh, sure. Tory and Skyler, even Jessica, had said, "You're family." But, in her experience, family wasn't synonymous with love.

I've fallen in love with you.

Indecision paralyzed her.

Her cell phone rang and she stared at it. The caller was identified as restricted. Maybe it was Bridgette. Maybe she hadn't really left. Maybe it wasn't too late. She grabbed the phone and dashed for the door, flinging it open as she put the phone to her ear.

"Hello? Bridgette?"

"No. It's Claire. I hope that's not too disappointing."

The spot where Bridgette's rental car had been parked the night before was empty. She was gone.

If you really need to get on that bull tomorrow, we're done.

But she had a shot at the national finals. That's what she wanted, right? Bridgette said she loved her, but she'd also left. Again. She frowned. Everything was getting all jumbled up. She needed time to think.

"Ryder, honey. Are you still there?"

"Oh, uh, yeah. Hi. Are you in DC?"

"No, I've been in Miami for the past three weeks, but I'm headed to the West Coast and I've just boarded a flight to Dallas, where I have an overnight layover. Are you back in Texas?"

"Yeah. The rodeo is in Mesquite, on the outskirts of Dallas, this week. It's the last big event before the National Finals Rodeo in Vegas."

"Are you working tonight?"

"I ride tomorrow." She scanned the parking lot one more time. Hell, she didn't even remember what model car Bridgette was driving.

"Then you're free. I'll book a room at the same hotel as last time and text you with my room number. Gotta run. The stewardess is having a fit for me to turn off my cell. See you tonight."

"Claire, wait." But she had already hung up. Crap.

A few drinks and sex with a beautiful woman *was* her standard pre-rodeo procedure, but she didn't want to spend the night with another woman. She wanted Bridgette to come back. Didn't she?

She closed the door and stood in the middle of her living room. The condo seemed empty now. Bridgette had filled it with her presence, her scent, her heat. The spot on the floor where her purse had been, the chair where she'd sat in the kitchen—all empty now.

Upstairs, she flopped across the bed to stare at the ceiling. That was a mistake. Bridgette's perfume, mixed with the unmistakable scent of their lovemaking, was even stronger here. She couldn't think clearly with so many reminders of her.

She pulled on her boots and grabbed a jacket. When she climbed into her truck, she paused to take in the lone tree that she shared with the adjoining condo. The leaves had turned almost overnight to a brilliant red. Things were changing in her world and she couldn't seem to stop it. The things that had been enough weren't sufficient now.

Her thoughts shifted to Cherokee Falls, surrounded by mountains and thick hardwood forests. It would be an amazing autumn palette right now. An image flashed of her and Bridgette riding a trail through that glorious display of color.

She paused at the exit of the parking lot. Could she still catch Bridgette before she boarded a plane? What she felt for Bridgette was confusing, much more terrifying than a two-thousand-pound bull. She sighed and turned her truck toward Mesquite.

❖

The nonstop flight leaving immediately for Richmond was expensive, but the sprint through security to board on time kept Bridgette from second-guessing her abrupt exit. Now that she was buckled in and the plane was taxiing down the runway, doubt began to creep in.

Issuing an ultimatum went against everything in her. She believed in live and let live. If other people needed something, who was she to deny it? Tory had needed Leah, not her. The dean had needed her to head the auction committee. Her brother had needed to run with the bulls.

But this was about what she needed. Her thoughts returned to the night before. God, she needed Marc's passion. She also needed her trust.

Marc was fighting her own battle. Could she open her heart to another person who might leave her? Did Marc care enough about her to try?

Despite my best efforts to stay away, I've fallen in love with you, damn it.

Christ, that sounded like she already regretted what she was feeling. Would it have made a difference if she'd said, "I'll love you forever, but I need you to be safe?"

She wasn't sure, not sure at all. She was absolutely certain, though, that she could only give her heart to someone who would protect it.

Ryder sat alone on the very top row in one corner of the Resistol Arena. The noise of the crowd and the announcer filled the air around her. The smell of cowhide and horse sweat mixed with the dust of the arena floor.

She sipped her favorite single-malt Scotch. As a member of the 8 Second Club, she had a seat reserved on the arena floor. She also could have found plenty of company and alcohol in the club's lounge. But she wanted to be alone with her thoughts, so she sat just below the rafters and drank from her flask.

She absently watched a cowboy fling himself from his horse to grab a young steer's horns and flip him onto his back in the steer-wrestling event.

You need to be honest with yourself about why you really need to do this.

It was more than the thrill. Taking chances was all she'd known since that first reckless ride on Kate Parker's stallion. She was addicted to it.

Constant restlessness had driven her from one job to the next, from one place to another. She'd never stopped to reflect on what compelled her to seek increasingly dangerous jobs, but she realized now that her life had been a headlong dash down a perilous path with no thought to where or how it could end.

When she'd worked as a polo rider in Florida, one of the old grooms there had lost his grandson in a gang fight. Why, she asked him, do young men join gangs and throw away their futures? "Because they see no value in their lives," he said. "They have no dreams, no long-range plans, and nobody who cares."

Did she have a plan for her life?

She watched the cowboys milling around the rough stock pens below her. They loved this, but did she? Would she grow bored like she'd tired of so many other past adventures? If she survived this one, what would be her next test? Swimming with sharks?

She had no dream to pursue.

Tory had achieved her dream of becoming a veterinarian. Skyler had many dreams and achievements—a gold medal, a job she loved, and now a family to care for.

Ryder had no one who cared.

Not really. The women she bedded didn't care. Her agent only cared about the money she made for him. Her fans would forget her as soon as she quit the rodeo.

She took another sip and closed her eyes as the liquor burned down her throat. Her mind filled with the vision of Bridgette, breath-stealingly beautiful, sleeping in her bed. The memory was so vivid, she could almost feel Bridgette's soft, warm skin on her lips, under her fingertips. Her heart fluttered and her belly clenched.

Bridgette cared enough to ask her to stop, to think about her future. What would happen if she did make a long-range plan, one that included Bridgette?

She sighed. Risking her heart was a hundred times more terrifying than anything she'd done before.

She drained the last of the Scotch and groaned when she stood to slide the flask into her back pocket. Her right shoulder and leg full of metal were still sore from the bronc riding earlier that week. She limped slowly down the steps.

Swimming with sharks was sounding better and better.

Bridgette's cell phone chirped and vibrated when it powered up as she walked through the Richmond airport to where she'd parked her car. She glanced at the screen. Twelve text messages, fifteen missed calls, and five voice mails. Most were from Lydia. A couple were from Dean Blanchard. The others were from a variety of people, all connected to the auction.

Flying to Texas had been insane. The auction was tomorrow night and she had a million details to double-check. Still, she didn't regret one minute of the time she'd spent with Marc. She didn't even regret confessing that she was in love with her. If she had to change anything, she'd take a do-over on how she'd phrased that confession. But she wasn't perfect and she'd done her best. The rest was up to Marc.

Ryder knocked on the door and stared down at the arena dust still covering her boots. She'd considered going home to change. But she hated the Dallas downtown traffic, and it was easier to hop on the interstate that looped north of the city to reach Claire's hotel near the Dallas-Forth Worth airport.

She looked up when the door jerked open.

Claire was gorgeous in faded jeans and a simple white tank top that showed off her Miami tan. Her blond hair was loose around her shoulders and her eyes even bluer than Ryder had remembered.

"Hi."

"Hi, sexy. I sure was dreading this layover until I found out you'd be here." Claire smiled as she ran her fingers through Ryder's newly cropped hair. "I love it. It makes you deadly cute." Her hands fell to the buttons on Ryder's shirt. "In fact, you look so dangerous, I'm afraid I'm going to have to strip-search you."

Chapter Twenty-three

D on't forget to pick up our dresses from the dry cleaners before noon," Lydia said, adjusting the hang of a canvas for the hundredth time. "The woman said they close early today. Who ever heard of dry cleaners closing early on Saturdays?"

"This isn't New York City. Everybody who lives here knows what time they close. Mr. Early has to get over to the high school to referee intramural basketball on Saturday afternoons." Bridgette pulled her eyes from the stormy abstract displayed in the studio. "I thought I told you the paintings from the small studio were not for sale."

"That's the only one. It's not up to you. William, uh, Dean Blanchard thinks we should include it. The agreement specifically states we can sell any painting we found in the house."

Bridgette pressed her lips together. This one was too private for public eyes. She walked over to her purse and pulled out her seldom-used checkbook. She scribbled out an amount and signed it.

"I'm exercising my privilege as chairwoman of the committee and claiming this one pre-auction." She handed the check to Lydia.

"Holy shit! That painting shows promise, Bridge, but twenty-five thousand dollars? It's only worth ten or fifteen max."

"Just give the money to Jonathan Frank. He's the treasurer for this fund-raiser."

She avoided Lydia's penetrating stare, taking the artwork she'd just purchased from the wall and substituting one of her own in its place. She'd been up most of the night painting it. She preferred oil over watercolors, but she needed something that would dry fast.

"You went after her, didn't you? That's why I couldn't get in touch with you until yesterday afternoon."

It was useless to deny it. "Yes. I flew to Dallas to try to stop her."

"Stop her?"

"She rides bulls in the rodeo."

"No shit? I saw that once, on one of those cable sports channels. Damn, those chaps they wear are criminally sexy." Lydia wiggled her eyebrows and grinned, then frowned. "Wait, I didn't think women did that sort of thing."

"That's because most women are too smart." She instantly regretted the venom in her words. It revealed too much, and Lydia's expression made it clear that she'd noticed.

"Did she come back with you? She's your date tonight, right?"

"Looks like I'm going stag." She meant to sound flippant but failed miserably.

"Oh, honey. You really care about her, don't you?"

She nodded. Her vision blurred with tears as Lydia's arm slipped around her shoulders in a hug.

"Tell me exactly what happened."

She pressed the heels of her hands to her eyes and took a deep breath before dropping them. "I tried to reason with her."

Lydia huffed. "Obviously, I need to remind you that, as a woman, you have much better weapons in your arsenal."

Despite her distress, she chuckled. "Okay. First, I fucked her brains out."

"That's my girl. What else?"

She closed her eyes. She could see Marc standing in her condo, soft and sexy in faded jeans and a half-buttoned forest-green shirt that complemented her dark-chocolate eyes.

"I told her I've fallen in love with her," she whispered.

"Oh, my God." Lydia released Bridgette's shoulders to take her hands and squeeze them. She was the only one who could possibly know how much this had cost her.

"Then I told her that if she gets on that bull she's supposed to ride today, we're finished."

"And she refused?" Lydia's brow furrowed. "I've seen the way she looks at you. I can't believe she'd pick a smelly old cow over you." Lydia didn't question the ultimatum. She understood why Bridgette was desperate for Ryder to do something else with her life.

Bridgette stared at her feet. "I was too afraid to wait for an answer. I left."

"You left? You told her to pick you or her job and then walked out?"

"Well, she didn't exactly stop me."

"Aww, honey. I'm sorry." Lydia wrapped her in a tight hug. "What can I do to help?"

She returned the affection and stepped back, gathering herself. "Just help me get through this damned auction. Then clear some time for me when the semester ends next month. I want to go to a sunny beach somewhere for the holidays."

"That's the best idea you've had in years. Count me in."

Bach blasted from the Bose speakers in Ryder's RV, filling her ears and her mind as she tried to drown out the voices that continued to argue in her head. She wouldn't have any room for doubt when she lowered herself onto the back of the eighteen-hundred-pound bull she'd drawn and nodded for the chute to open. A few hundred pounds smaller than average, he'd be more agile and a fierce ride. She had to find her focus.

She stepped into the shower before the water had time to heat. She was tired and needed the cold jolt. Claire had been great. Really great.

Bridgette had changed everything. She filled Ryder with hope. And she filled her with fear. Ryder's easy-come, easy-go life had belly-rolled like a bucking bull and was twirling her, tilting her, sucking her into a well of emotion she was afraid would drown her.

When she had knocked on that hotel-room door, part of her wanted to be swept away in the familiar dance of hot, no-boundaries sex. It felt safe. It felt easy. It felt wrong. Before Claire had reached the last button on Ryder's shirt, she knew she couldn't do it.

Claire was disappointed when she stopped her hands but respected her dilemma. She'd changed clothes and demanded, instead, that she take her to an expensive restaurant and tell her everything. Claire didn't judge. She didn't offer advice. She just listened. After they had eaten and she was talked out, Claire clasped her hand and held it to her lips in a brief kiss.

"If I was inclined to settle down with one woman, it would be somebody like you. But I value my freedom—a girl at every airport, so to speak. That may change one day if I meet the right person, but not yet. Apparently you have met a woman who has changed that for you."

Claire had risen from her chair but motioned for her to remain seated. "I'll grab a cab back to the hotel. Thank you for dinner." She smiled. "And the best sex I've ever had." Claire bent to kiss her cheek. "You're so sweet. I hope you get everything you want, when you finally admit to yourself what that is. And if doesn't work out, you have my number."

They both knew she wouldn't call again.

The water in the shower began to warm, and she flexed to loosen the muscles still sore from the bronc and her night with Bridgette.

She closed her eyes and visualized the upcoming ride. She breathed deeply as it played through her mind, and, when the mental ride was done, she turned off the water and stepped out of the shower to begin her ritual.

She dried off, wrapped her torso, carefully taped her right arm and legs, pulled on her compression undergarments, then began to dress. With each layer to protect her body, she also pulled on her mental armor to sharpen her focus.

By the time she walked from the RV to the arena with the braided leather bull rope slung over her shoulder, she was barely aware of the fans who stopped her to ask for her autograph on a program or an article of clothing. She was almost surprised when the rodeo stockman took the bull rope from her and the announcer was introducing her as the next rider.

The bull she had drawn was young and restless in the chute. Hannibal was the grandson of Dillinger, one of rodeo's most notorious bucking bulls.

"He's pretty rank today. Better let me spot you while you get situated," the old stock steward said.

She nodded and drew her new piece of equipment over her head—a hockey-style helmet with a full-face mask. Sweat trickled down her temple. She longed for her Stetson but couldn't completely ignore the doctor's warning about the consequences of another concussion. She tightened the chinstrap and swung over the top rail.

She braced her feet on the sides of the chute as the bull tossed his head and tried to buck in the small space. She waited for him to settle then stroked his back with her boot. He snorted and banged against the sides, so she waited again.

"Good thing she's got two more rides after this one, folks, because it looks like this bull is in a particularly bad mood today and doesn't plan for this one to beat the buzzer." The crowd tittered at the announcer's comment and then grew quiet as they anticipated the break from the chute.

Ryder slid onto the broad back and winced when Hannibal threw himself back and forth in an effort to crush her legs against the sides of the chute. Damn, that hurt. She yanked the bull rope tight around the animal's chest and he stilled, tensed like a rattlesnake waiting to strike.

She slipped her fingers into the handhold and drew the braided leather tail of the bull rope tight across her gloved hand before looping it around and across her palm again. She curled her fingers down and pounded them into the rosin-coated rope with her free hand.

She sucked in a deep breath. The odor of sweat and bull filled her lungs, and she smiled. She didn't have any doubt or residual apprehension over her last experience with a bull, the one that had sent her to the hospital. She could do this. She knew it, and in eight seconds this bull named after a serial killer would know it.

She raised her free hand and stared down at the bull's horns.

No fear. Her confidence and anticipation swelled. She could do this.

The gate steward tensed for her nod.

Chapter Twenty-four

Tuxedoed men and women dressed in a dazzling display of cocktail dresses milled about the house, still filling the large studio upstairs and all of the downstairs rooms even though the actual auction had concluded more than an hour earlier.

"Ah, the woman of the hour." William Blanchard's gray eyes were jubilant. He reached for Bridgette's hand and squeezed it in an unprecedented display of affection. "My dear, I can't thank you enough for what you've done here today."

"I can claim only a small part of the credit," she said. "The rest of the committee, our students, and so many others have worked very hard to make this happen."

It was a huge success. In the end, catering and postage to mail out the catalogue of what was offered had been the only real expense. The auctioneer donated his time to the cause. Lydia and several other gallery owners, who regularly sold paintings by the contributing artists, funded the biggest expense—compiling and printing the catalogue. Art-department student volunteers worked as wait staff, parking valets, and auction assistants.

"Nonetheless, you steered it all. Jonathan has only preliminary figures, but he's sure we've collected twice what we had hoped. It will be a more than adequate start on the endowment, and this auction also has put our little school in the international limelight. I've had to employ an administrative temp just to help answer all the inquiries we're getting from prospective students."

"I'm so glad, Dean Blanchard. I really love teaching."

D. Jackson Leigh

"Please, it's William. I may be dean of the school, but you are its savior. I truly am in your debt."

"I'm going to be in debt, too, when Laura adds up what she bought." A tall woman with short, curly white hair and laughing blue eyes extended her hand. "Hello, William. I thought that was you standing here, grinning like the Cheshire cat."

"Kate, so good to see you. Where have you been keeping yourself?"

"Greece, mostly. Laura and I are enjoying traveling now that we're retired and have dumped our responsibilities on the kids. My new passion is sailing on the Mediterranean."

"We've missed you at the club. It's been rather quiet without you around."

Kate Parker chuckled and held out her hand to a petite woman who was approaching with her arm linked in Jessica's. "Laura's itching for a round of golf, so you may see us there next week."

Jessica greeted Bridgette with a hug. "I see Kate has found my favorite artist. I've been waiting all evening to say hello. Every time I could catch sight of you in the crowd, someone would whisk you away."

"Sorry. I did see Tory and Leah earlier. Is Skyler with you?"

"No, she's home with the baby. She insisted Leigh is too young to leave with a sitter, but it's really that she hates these formal events. I let her get away with it, though, because I wanted to buy some art without her having a heart attack over the prices. Have you met my moms?"

"I'm so sorry. I haven't had a chance to introduce her yet." William frowned at his social blunder, but Bridgette smiled to let him know she wasn't offended.

"Bridgette LeRoy, artist extraordinaire and the organizer of this event, these are my moms—Kate and Laura Parker."

"Hello," Bridgette said, extending her hand. "I've heard so much about you two. I'm pleased to at last meet you in person."

"Don't believe anything Skyler says." Kate's handshake was firm.

"I love the painting you did of Skyler," Laura said. "She nearly had a heart attack, though, when Jess showed it to me."

Kate's laughter boomed. "I had to sit on her, just so Laura could go in their bedroom to see it."

They were referring to a nude portrait of Skyler that Jessica had commissioned Bridgette to paint from a photograph.

"She's not usually modest," Jessica said. "But you have to admit it's a little intimidating for your mother-in-law to see a picture of you naked."

Bridgette winked. "I would think so." She couldn't tell Jessica that Skyler had called her about a new commission, a photograph she'd taken of Jessica breastfeeding their daughter. It was to be a Christmas present.

Laura turned to William. "Kate and I would love it if you and Martha could join us for a game of golf next week."

William beamed. "I'm sure she'd like that, too. I'll get her to call you to settle on a tee time."

While William launched into an explanation of recent changes to the golf course, Jessica sidled close to Bridgette.

"I was hoping Ryder would be here," she said quietly.

She shook her head. "She's in Dallas. I was hoping…" She was grateful that the golf-course analysis concluded so Jessica couldn't press for more.

Kate slapped William on the back. "Well, I need to write a check so we can go rescue Leigh before Skyler has her out in the barn saddling up her first pony."

"It was a pleasure to meet you, Bridgette," Laura said.

Jessica gave Bridgette another brief hug. "Dinner at our place Wednesday, and no excuses this time."

"Wednesday sounds good," she said.

She loved her friends, but the emotional turmoil and lack of sleep over the past few days had exhausted her. She wandered upstairs where the crowd in the studio had finally thinned to only a few people. The artwork would remain on display until Monday, when each piece would be individually crated for delivery. She browsed through it, stopping before the watercolor she'd painted on a whim the previous night.

Marc's dark eyes looked back at her. Her left arm curled up to embrace Wind Walker, her hand flat against his beautifully arched neck as he rubbed his head against her shoulder and sniffed her other hand for a treat. She had painted it from her memory of the day she saw them together in the pasture. The only exception was Marc's hair, cut in the short, spiky style she had admired only a day ago in Dallas.

"Hey, I've been looking for you." Lydia spoke quietly and snaked her arm around Bridgette's waist. "You okay?"

"Things here are winding down. I think I am, too."

"Well, you should go home and sleep until Monday, when we have to start packing everything up." Lydia released her and kissed her briefly on the cheek. "You've got the loft to yourself. I've been invited to a sleepover, so you won't have to worry about entertaining me."

She chuckled and shook her head, her gaze still on the painting. "I should have known you'd pick up somebody tonight."

Lydia glanced toward the door. "The night isn't over. There's still a chance for you, too."

"Good night, Lydia."

The sound of Lydia's heels clicking cross the hardwood floor had barely faded before she was again immersed in her thoughts.

One voice in her head screamed for her to check the Internet to see if Marc had survived today's ride. Another voice calmly told her to let it go, let Marc go. She ignored them both and, instead, closed her eyes and opened the memory of their last night of passion—Marc's head thrown back, breasts heaving and heart beating wildly against her cheek.

She opened her eyes and stared at her painting. Well, not hers any more. Someone had paid an extravagant sum to purchase it. It was time to say good-bye, to the painting and to her hope that Marc would choose her.

She lifted her hand to touch the face she had come to love.

"I'm certain the buyer of that piece would not appreciate fingerprints on it."

Her heart leapt into her throat and she whirled to find Marc at her side, wearing a cocky smile and the sexiest tailored tuxedo she'd ever seen on a woman.

"In fact, since I'm the new owner of that portrait, I can guarantee it."

Her thoughts rapid-fired, ricocheting in her head. Marc was safe. Marc was here. Why had she come? Damn, she was gorgeous.

"Marc."

"Shhh. You've had your chance to talk. It's my turn."

Marc took her hand to lead her out of the studio and down the hall to the bedroom. She closed the door and locked it.

They stopped next to the bed where they'd made love before. It seemed like ages ago now. Marc kissed her hand, then turned it to press her mouth against the inside of her sensitive wrist. Her gaze was a soft caress.

"You are so beautiful," Marc said. "Don't move. Just listen." She stepped back and began to slowly undress as she spoke.

"There's one perfect moment in bull riding." She unfastened the gold brooch that substituted for a bow tie and slid it into her pocket before dropping her jacket to the floor.

"You'd think that moment would be when the buzzer goes off and you know you've ridden that animal for a full eight seconds." Marc worked the pearl studs loose from her shirt, revealing her bare breasts.

"But that's not it." Her shirt joined the jacket on the floor, and she toed off her boots and socks.

"It's that long second when that bull rope is tight around one hand and your other is held high over your head. You're staring down at the bull's horns and you feel him between your legs, coiled to buck as soon as you give the nod." Marc's hands went to the zipper of her pants.

"That's when the perfect moment happens. You're perched on a precipice. When that gate opens, there's no turning back. But it's in that moment that you know." She stripped her pants and underwear off in one movement.

"You know with absolute certainty whether you can do it." She stood before Bridgette fully exposed.

"Marc."

"Just listen." She knelt and gently removed Bridgette's shoes then stood again. "I was there today."

Bridgette shivered when Marc's lips found her neck as she reached around and slid the zipper down on her simple black dress.

"I was one perfect moment away from riding a bull named after a serial killer. That's when I knew." Marc smiled when Bridgette's dress dropped to the floor and revealed she also was braless. She lowered Bridgette's panties and hose and tossed them across the room.

They were both naked now.

"I knew I wasn't there to satisfy my agent or my sponsors or my fans. I was there so I could know for sure that I wasn't afraid after the last bull nearly killed me."

Bridgette's vision blurred with tears as her heart emptied of hope. Marc had needed to ride that bull more than she needed to love her.

"No. Don't cry." Marc's lips brushed her cheek. When she lifted her head, Marc's gaze was full of affection.

"Then a second epiphany came to me as perfect as a pearl." She raised an eyebrow and smiled. "And I climbed out of that chute and told them I was sorry, but I had a plane to catch."

"You…you didn't ride?"

"No. Not today or any day in the future."

Relief and, at the same time, regret flooded through her. She sagged with the weight of it and Marc caught her, lowering her gently to the bed. She sobbed against Marc's shoulder.

"I'm sorry. I'm so sorry. I never meant for my weakness to cost you so much."

Marc's hands stroked her back as she held her. "No. It's okay. Really. It won't cost so much. I already know a guy who wants to buy the RV I take to rodeos."

She laughed, in spite of herself, and Marc smiled as she used the bedsheet to dry Bridgette's tears.

"I've never been in love before," Marc said. "I've never let myself." She shrugged. "I have abandonment issues. You should know that before you get involved with me."

"It's too late. I've already fallen for you."

"Ah. But I fell for you first. The morning after we made love in this room, I knew I was hopelessly lost." Marc kissed her again, her tongue teasing Bridgette's lips.

"Say it." She needed to hear it, needed to know it was true.

"I love you, Bridgette. I want to show you how much."

Marc kissed her gently, then deeply as she rolled her onto her back. Belly to belly, their hips fit together perfectly, and they shared breath and longing as their tongues met in an unhurried waltz.

Marc's thigh slid between hers and she moaned. A slow glide slicked her thigh with Marc's heat. Their breath quickened with each measured stroke until they could kiss no longer. Still, Marc held the steady pace, her hands finding Bridgette's breasts, her gaze capturing Bridgette's as their fervor mounted.

"I love you," Marc whispered.

"I need you," she gasped.

Hers to command, Marc thrust faster, bearing down harder as though to meld their flesh as well as their souls.

When they reached the precipice together, they shared that perfect moment when passion peaks for a few breathless seconds before it explodes and dissipates in waves of pleasure.

She lay panting, her heart dancing with Marc's in an erratic pounding staccato. When her sweat-slicked body began to cool, Marc rolled onto her side and drew the sheet up to cover them. They lay face to face, their legs still entwined.

Bridgette touched her fingers to Marc's cheek. "I can't believe we're lying here naked with a house full of art patrons milling around just outside our door."

"They're probably all gone now. I asked Lydia to do what she could to clear them out, then lock up when she left. I called her as soon as the jet I chartered left Dallas and I knew what time I'd land. She promised to put sheets on this bed and make sure you didn't leave before I could get here."

Bridgette frowned. "You had her cell number?"

"She got my number from your phone and texted me that day I came here and she was with you."

"That little minx. Wait until I get my hands around her neck."

"She never had a chance. You already had my heart."

Bridgette was quiet, sorting through all that had happened. She couldn't believe Marc was here and that she loved her. She studied her handsome face.

"You said you had a second epiphany."

Marc smiled. "I did."

"Want to share?"

"Everything with you."

Marc took her hand and pressed it against her chest to hold it there. She could feel the throb of her strong, steady heart.

"I realized I could do this," Marc said. "That I could trust someone again, trust you with my heart."

"I love you," she said, stroking the cheek under her fingertips. She couldn't stop touching her. "So, what will you do now?"

"Wind Walker has a lot of good stud years left, and I have this house and an empty stable out back. I was hoping to settle down with a sexy artist—if she'll have me—and maybe raise Arabians."

Her heart soared, but she pursed her lips as though she was thinking it over. "Your grandmother's studio does have perfect lighting." She pushed Marc onto her back and straddled her hips. "But—other than horses—I have to be your only ride."

"Only you."

"And I want a lot more than eight seconds."

Marc flashed the cocky grin that always made Bridgette's insides clench. "I *am* a professional rider. I'm thinking endurance may be my next venture."

About the Author

Jackson Leigh grew up barefoot and happy, swimming in farm ponds and riding rude ponies in rural south Georgia.

Her passion for writing led her quite accidentally to a career in journalism and North Carolina where she now feeds nightly off the adrenaline rush of breaking crime news and close deadlines.

She is a hopeless romantic with a deep-seated love for anything equine.

Friend her at facebook.com/d.jackson.leigh, follow her on Twitter @djacksonleigh or visit her website at www.djacksonleigh.com.

Books Available from Bold Strokes Books

Cut to the Chase by Lisa Girolami. Careful and methodical author Paige Randolph falls for brash and wild Hollywood actress, Avalon Randolph, but can these opposites find a happy middle ground in a town that never lives in the middle? (978-1-60282-783-7)

More Than Friends by Erin Dutton. Evelyn Fisher thinks she has the perfect role model for a long-term relationship, until her best friends, Kendall and Melanie, split up and all three women must reevaluate their lives and their relationships. (978-1-60282-784-4)

Every Second Counts by D. Jackson Leigh. Every second counts in Bridgette LeRoy's desperate mission to protect her heart and stop Marc Ryder's suicidal return to riding rodeo bulls. (978-1-60282-785-1)

Dirty Money by Ashley Bartlett. Vivian Cooper and Reese DiGiovanni just found out that falling in love is hard. It's even harder when you're running for your life. (978-1-60282-786-8)

Promises in Every Star edited by Todd Gregory. Acclaimed gay male erotica author Todd Gregory's definitive collection of short stories, including both classic and new works. (978-1-60282-787-5)

Wonderland by David-Matthew Barnes. After her mother's sudden death, Destiny Moore is sent to live with her two gay uncles on Avalon Cove, a mysterious island on which she uncovers a secret place called Wonderland, where love and magic prove to be real. (978-1-60282-788-2)

Sea Glass Inn by Karis Walsh. When Melinda Andrews commissions a series of mosaics by Pamela Whitford for her new inn, she doesn't expect to be more captivated by the artist than by the paintings. (978-1-60282-771-4)

The Awakening: A Sisters of Spirits novel by Yvonne Heidt. Sunny Skye has interacted with spirits her entire life, but when she runs into Officer Jordan Lawson during a ghost investigation, she discovers more than just facts in a missing girl's cold case file. (978-1-60282-772-1)

Murphy's Law by Yolanda Wallace. No matter how high you climb, you can't escape your past. (978-1-60282-773-8)

Blacker Than Blue by Rebekah Weatherspoon. Threatened with losing her first love to a powerful demon, vampire Cleo Jones is willing to break the ultimate law of the undead to rebuild the family she has lost. (978-1-60282-774-5)

Another 365 Days by KE Payne. Clemmie Atkins is back, and her life is more complicated than ever! Still madly in love with her girlfriend, Clemmie suddenly finds her life turned upside down with distractions, confessions, and the return of a familiar face... (978-1-60282-775-2)

Tricks of the Trade: Magical Gay Erotica, edited by Jerry L. Wheeler. Today's hottest erotica writers take you inside the sultry, seductive world of magicians and their tricks—professional and otherwise. (978-1-60282-781-3)

Straight Boy Roommate by Kevin Troughton. Tom isn't expecting much from his first term at University, but a chance encounter with straight boy Dan catapults him into an extraordinary, wild weekend of sex and self-discovery, which turns his life upside down, and leads him into his first love affair. (978-1-60282-782-0)

Silver Collar by Gill McKnight. Werewolf Luc Garoul is outlawed and out of control, but can her family track her down before a sinister predator gets there first? Fourth in the Garoul series. (978-1-60282-764-6)

The Dragon Tree Legacy by Ali Vali. For Aubrey Tarver time hasn't dulled the pain of losing her first love Wiley Gremillion, but she has to set that aside when her choices put her life and her family's lives in real danger. (978-1-60282-765-3)

The Midnight Room by Ronica Black. After a chance encounter with the mysterious and brooding Lillian Gray in the "midnight room" of The Griffin, a local lesbian bar, confident and gorgeous Audrey McCarthy learns that her bad-girl behavior isn't bulletproof. (978-1-60282-766-0)

Dirty Sex by Ashley Bartlett. Vivian Cooper and twins Reese and Ryan DiGiovanni stole a lot of money and the guy they took it from wants it back. Like now. (978-1-60282-767-7)

Raising Hell: Demonic Gay Erotica, edited by Todd Gregory. Hot stories of gay erotica featuring demons. (978-1-60282-768-4)

Pursued by Joel Gomez-Dossi. Openly gay college student Jamie Bradford becomes romantically involved with two men at the same time, and his hell begins when one of his boyfriends becomes intent on killing him. (978-1-60282-769-1)

The Storm by Shelley Thrasher. Rural East Texas. 1918. War-weary Jaq Bergeron and marriage-scarred musician Molly Russell try to salvage love from the devastation of the war abroad and natural disasters at home. (978-1-60282-780-6)

Crossroads by Radclyffe. Dr. Hollis Monroe specializes in short-term relationships but when she meets pregnant mother-to-be Annie Colfax, fate brings them together at a crossroads that will change their lives forever. (978-1-60282-756-1)